MY
ONLY
WIFE

jac jemc

DZANC
BOOKS

www.dzancbooks.org

Design by Steven Seighman

ISBN: 978-1-936873-68-5

First edition: April 2012

Printed in the United States of America

10 9 8 7 6 5 4 3 2 1

for my father and his first and only wife, my mother

That those who know her, know her less
The nearer her they get.
—Emily Dickinson
"What mystery pervades a well!"

Is this what you wanted? to live in a house
that is haunted by the ghost of you and me?
—Leonard Cohen
"Is This What You Wanted"

MY
ONLY
WIFE

1.

MY WIFE HAD A BEAUTIFUL, beautiful time.

My wife climbed staircases like a bull, but she descended them like a Duchamp painting, all blurred angles and motion.

She was a performer and a creator and an admirer and an artist. She always had a project. I'm sure many I never knew about.

My wife would catch sight of someone, something, an idea, even, and begin her process of admiration, of absorption, of alteration.

Yes, she admired every person she came into contact with. She dreamt of meeting all of them and adding their names to her list of accomplishments.

More than a list—she kept a database. Her records were intricate and precise and thorough, frighteningly so.

In her daytimes my wife climbed, in her evenings she descended.

This shift in direction was not an act of indecision, but of routine and route. My wife loved routine, fed on it, found reason for impulse in regularity. She had it all mapped out.

My wife was a clumsy acquaintance who lumbered through days. She talked to anyone within earshot. She made friends in her awkwardness.

She would trip, spilling the contents of her purse on a sidewalk, and then insist on buying the girl who helped her collect her scattered belongings a cup of coffee. The girl would end up sitting down with my wife, instantly beguiled, immediately disarmed. My wife would learn everything. She would ask questions that might have seemed otherwise uncomfortable coming from anyone else, but in the initial whirlwind that seemed to constitute the large majority of my wife, the girl would offer up her secrets with open palms, and, like that, my wife would be gone.

My wife would come home and recite the story of this girl into a tape recorder.

My wife created narratives to connect the facts.

My wife fell a lot. Even when she was climbing through her days, she was falling a bit along the way. At night there didn't appear to be far to drop. She was careful in the dark. She took fewer risks and recuperated for day. "The night," she used to say, "should be for rest and repair."

In the evening, my wife nursed her scraped palms, a chronic injury from stopping her tumbles with her hands.

In the morning she was ready to work again. I never knew her when she wasn't toiling away at something.

She seemed to be constantly anxious about finishing some project or another.

My wife spent a small portion of each evening recording. She rambled through other people's stories, never claiming them as her own, holding them at arm's length, archiving them but never possessing them.

But it was my wife who knew how important they were. It was my wife who told the stories the way they were meant to be told and made them available. Who found them and then gave them away, even if it was just to cassette tapes that she then stashed in a closet.

These stories were not about anyone other than my wife. That's what I discovered. I found that when you got to the bottom of them it was my wife that remained the essence, that I could scrape from the sides of the crucible. The rest was filler.

2.

My wife was a waitress.

When people asked her what she did, she proudly said that word. She liked it and she didn't want to give it up. She thought being a waitress made her sound romantic. She liked people imagining her running around with a little black apron and her hair falling in stray pieces down the back of her neck and dusting her high cheekbones.

She never said she worked in a restaurant. She liked the way "waitress" hissed out her mouth more easily than the blunt alternative of "server." She thought "server" sounded clunky and imprecise.

She also didn't like the way "waiter" was being used as gender-neutral. She rather *liked* being defined by her gender. My wife said, "Obviously, I'm a woman. 'Server' is fine for want ads, but a 'waitress' is what I am in conversation."

She preferred whatever came clearest, prettiest when spoken aloud.

My wife could have done anything, but she became a waitress. She liked having a job she could leave behind at the end of the day. It left the rest of her life stress-free so she could fulfill her creative ambitions: telling stories, decorating haunted houses, researching art history, eventually painting.

"But you went to college!" people would say.

"Oh, I'm probably putting my education to better use than you." She'd challenge them with a raised eyebrow and refuse further explanation.

I made the mistake once of telling her she didn't have to wait tables if she didn't want to. She looked at me, her eyes dead. "No shit. You should know better than anyone that I like it! And, what? I'm going to rely entirely on you? Let you support me? What if something happens to you? What will I do then? I need to do real work, real, physical labor. I have too much energy not to. Anyway, this allows us to put a little extra into the retirement fund." She felt bad for snapping, ruffled my hair to soften the moment.

My wife's clumsiness made for some good stories at work. She was a waitress at a hip, uptown restaurant where she was required to wear a spotless, white tee shirt and anything else she wanted.

At the end of the day my wife's tee shirt was anything but white. We bought masses of men's white undershirts and gallons of bleach to keep her spic and span for the beginnings of her shifts.

She would come home and strip herself of the soiled white tee, and put on one of her favorites: an old band tee shirt frayed into oblivion, one of her father's ancient softball jerseys, a cut-up child's sweatshirt printed with a vocabulary of dinosaurs.

She would settle into one of these shirts and begin scrubbing her work shirt in the bathroom sink, rubbing the fabric until the bleach-infused water left her hands raw.

I'd visit her at the restaurant and ask to be seated at one of her tables. My wife would introduce me to her co-workers. They'd shake my hand, greeting me with wide-eyed, friendly smiles. They always seemed to be searching my face for something. We'd make small talk for a minute, my wife and I smiling so proudly at her fellow servers, until each one had to hurry off to check on a table.

My wife's customers adored her. "One hour of bliss," they would say, then request her when they returned.

My wife took group photographs with skill.

She was a nonchalant winker who equally eyed the ladies and the gentleman. She'd get monumental tips.

Even the women my wife inevitably spilled glasses of very red wine on came back and greeted her with warm hugs.

People thanked my wife for her forthright opinions of the menu and for providing the deciding vote in petty arguments. People loved the way she influenced their meals and my wife loved being a part of their evenings out. She adored her job. She could work when she pleased and she got to meet new people every day.

When the hour was up, two hours if there were several courses served, the diners would gather their belongings and smile warmly at my wife on their way out.

My wife would go to pick up another table's order from the kitchen, and in all the frantic sizzling and scrambling and splashing, a buzzer would sound.

Something was finished in the nick of time.

3.

MY WIFE WORE TROUSERS.

She never said she disliked skirts; she just never wore them.

I was always aware of what my wife was wearing. Her clothing not only complemented her, it seemed integral to her personality. She filled her clothes the way one fills one's skin: exactly. It was as difficult to imagine her without skin as it was to imagine her undressed.

When she bared herself, her clothing falling slack on the floor around her the way one's skin peels away from one's flesh in a ripe tear, the sight was shocking: a bit grotesque, beautiful in its secrecy, riveting.

My wife was willowy. Not willowy in the way people commonly think of the word, but in a weeping willow sort of way. My wife was narrow. Her shoulders lacked breadth. There was a weight and direction to her slenderness. My wife's body was an arrow. There wasn't much to her, but what was there seemed to move towards the earth. The gravity of my wife could be overwhelming.

I was not the type to notice what people wore, but setting eyes on my wife educated me. I learned to look at her, and eventually I learned to see her.

There was a theatricality to her way of dressing that made heads turn.

She was a stunning woman and much credit was due to her physical presence alone. You didn't need to hear her utter a word to realize that in the midst of whatever was bubbling around her, she was a strong and calm pillar pushing its heft into the earth, ready to hoist any weight.

She was not born with a flawless face. Her eyes were noticeably asymmetrical, one larger than the other. My wife's ears stood at different heights, and only one side of her mouth tended to turn up naturally, so she seemed to be perpetually smirking at the world. She looked like she was always in on a joke.

These pants my wife wore had very wide legs. She liked to wear many layers to bulk up her frame.

She liked structure in her clothing.

Or maybe "architecture" is a better word. She liked angles and excess fabric in unexpected places. She like frayed edges and thinned spots.

When she bought a new shirt she dug into a drawer and took out her wire brushes and her sandpaper. She rubbed at hems and snipped tiny cuts into seams. My wife wouldn't wait for clothing to get old on its own.

She was eager to age. She spoke often of how she wanted grey hair more than anything.

I suggested once that she dye it and she said that would be false.

I reminded her of how she pretended to age her clothing.

She replied, "Oh, that's different. That's extra-corporeal."

My wife wanted to earn herself grey hair.

My wife could have a sense of humor, too. She would pull on opera-length satin gloves, a tiara, pearls, sunglasses, all very *Breakfast at Tiffany's*, but combined with her wide-legged pants and her gamut of worn-thin tee shirts, she was often eyed as being a bit off. I adored her oddities. My wife was magnificent and content in her whimsy.

The playfulness of her dress and the weight of her physicality made her entirely striking. Her graceful form and her clumsy movements seemed logical. Such an extreme in one respect, expected, in fact, *required* the opposite intensity to balance it.

She would enter with an elegant flourish and trip on the entrance mat, all grace erased by the pull of gravity that brought her back down.

4.

SHE WAS MY ONLY WIFE and I accepted her for all that she was, all quirks, all inconsistencies and unexpected preferences.

My wife hated mall jewelry stores more than most anything.

Sure she was exaggerating, people would make suggestions of what she must hate more. It was never long before my wife would admit, resignedly, that she hated war more, she hated child-abuse more. My wife claimed once, in a dinner party discussion, that she did indeed hate television more than mall jewelry stores, but I suspect she was just keeping up appearances on that one.

If you'd seen my wife in a mall, near one of its jewelry stores, you would know the truth.

My wife and I had never visited a mall together before we were married.

I loved that we could avoid it without talking about it. I thought I had found one of the only women who disliked malls. I was right, but it wasn't because she hated the capitalism in the air or disliked the activity of shopping.

I found out the real reason the day I proposed. I didn't feel the need to be creative. My wife was not a fan of rote romantic gestures. She was happy with simple straightforwardness. She liked intimacy and romanticism when they were genuinely inspired. She hated Valentine's Day. She despised roses. I was nervous the very act of proposing might annoy her. I didn't want to push my limits and do something grand, like taking her up in a hot air balloon.

That night we were reading in our apartment. I watched her read for a while, something I enjoyed doing. She mouthed the words as she read. She'd majored in theater in college and had grown accustomed to evaluating language through its sound. This was one of the reasons she loved to talk to people. This is why she didn't write the stories down at the end of her day. This is why my wife felt those tales needed to be spoken. She liked being a medium. She thought the stories became fraught with error when she retold them and she thought these second-hand mistakes were an inevitable addition to the evolution of the tales.

I'd watch my wife read, because she had a funny voice. She didn't add air to any of the syllables she read, but I watched her mouth twist around words in a way entirely her own. I imagined what Tolstoy sounded like with the crackled warp of my wife's reedy speech. I watched her shape her lips around all the poetry in each issue of *The Paris Review*. She like to take night classes and for three months I watched her silently project the laws of physics at the back wall of our living room.

She didn't read aloud because she didn't want to listen to *other* people read aloud. She feared if she began to read aloud, other people might as well, and then she would have to compete to hear her own voice. If she read and only mouthed the words, she could imagine what the words sounded like through muscle memory and the choreography of her lips.

On that night I was to propose, I watched her read until she looked up and smiled with a little bit of sheepish guilt, having been caught at this habit of hers. She didn't ask me what I was doing or what I was looking at. When she looked up is when I asked her to be my wife. She smiled again. My wife, skeptical, said, "Are you sure?"

I nodded. Of course I was sure. She knew, and yet still she asked. I was practical and predictable.

"You didn't think up the idea this moment?" My wife searched for a lie, knew the truth was plain.

In response to this question I reached into my jeans pocket and pulled out the little box. I popped the box open facing me and turned it so she could see the ring.

My wife wrinkled her nose and looked away.

"Is that from the mall?"

I was confused. She shivered and pulled her feet up to hug her legs to her chest. I nodded.

"You're going to think I'm nuts." My wife couldn't look in the direction of the little grey velvet box. "I will marry you. Of course, I will marry you. I will be your wife, but return the ring. *Now* would be best."

"You don't like it?"

"I know I'm crazy to say this, but there is nothing, seriously, nothing, I hate more than mall jewelry stores. You had no idea, I know. They make me…" I could see her struggle to find words, like she was suppressing a gag. She grunted. "Return it and go to an antique store and pick me something old and—imperfect. Something that has a little history."

I might have been hurt, but my wife was honest. She was kind, and she wouldn't say this because she didn't want to marry me. My wife appeared to be genuinely put-off.

She told me to return the emptiness of that ring to where I had gotten it.

She said, "You can bargain down the price in antique stores. Value is negotiable."

My wife said, "Things are unapologetically broken and incomplete in antique stories."

She said, "Be careful of the suited men with sharp, bright teeth in the mall who will try and talk you into an exchange."

My wife said, "Give me wood and fiber any day."

It wasn't late when I proposed. The mall was still open. I kissed her forehead and she smiled weakly. I'd never seen her smile with anything but strength.

I needed something to send me out. "You'll be my wife, though, right?"

With ease that sailed me to the mall, my wife said, "More than anything."

On the way to the store I phoned my father. I told him about the engagement. My dad asked me to put my wife on the phone. I told him she wasn't with me and that I was heading to the mall.

He asked why. I explained and he was confused. "Couldn't she wear the ring until you found another? Why won't she come to pick out a new one at the store with you? A ring is a ring."

I tried to explain that the ring was not the problem, but where it had come from. I tried to tell him that if I was going to spend the rest of my life with this woman I wasn't going to mar this day by forcing a ring on her that she hated.

I could practically hear the shrug of his shoulders over the phone before he digressed, "I'm happy for you. Send her my congratulations."

I parked the car in the lot and ran into the mall to explain the situation one more time.

I was delirious with joy. She had said she would be my wife.

5.

My wife didn't always find it easy or enjoyable to tell people's stories to that tape recorder. Some of the stories my wife collected were difficult.

On the evenings when this was the case she'd come home and put on a record. My wife and I only owned an old record player with a radio dial. I often offered to buy us a newer stereo but she forbade it. She said she had come to require the warp that vinyl records inevitably developed. It was like sleeping by the ocean; the subtle waves in the sound made each song a lullaby. She said, "A rocking chair couldn't work half so well."

Most commonly my wife put on old soul records she let sit by the radiator too long. They'd distort in and out, the sound twisting out of shape as she lay on the couch in a daze, letting the music bend around her while she tried to grasp how to tell a story.

My wife never told her stories for sensational effect. She liked to tell them in a way that would make them quiet and interesting. She wanted people to lean in. She liked to foreshadow huge events to come. She did this even when the stories were simple and straightforward. She gave hints when there was nothing to hint at.

The way the people told the stories to my wife would be out of order in the least interesting way. Often these acquaintances tended to share with my wife the hardest bit of their life first.

There was a sense that my wife could handle it, that telling her might lessen the blow each time these people would think about the event in the future.

There was a warm openness to my wife in the beginning of the story, like she was making some kind sacrifice to take on such a burden.

My wife never directly asked someone to tell his story, but she was adept at gently steering the conversation.

In the beginning my wife seemed generous, but by the end there was hunger.

She needed those stories to be told as much as the teller needed to relay them.

When my wife returned home, she would sit on the couch and evaluate how a listener wanted to be teased, eased into a story.

My wife would flip the arm of the record player all the way to the left to click it off. She didn't have one of those fancy little mini-tape recorders. She had one of the bulky ones that were about the size of a hardcover novel, with a slide-out handle. She clicked the RECORD button and spoke.

Sometimes she talked for only a short amount of time: not everyone was open with their lives, not everyone was aware of what was fascinating about themselves. Usually my wife could seek it out, but this is not to say there weren't exceptions.

Sometimes my wife would go on for over an hour. She would carry on and carry on.

Usually she clocked in around twenty minutes.

What seemed most fascinating about my wife's project, as she tried to explain it to me once in the beginning, was that she never included herself in the story. She never interjected how something made her feel or how she felt she was affected.

On the nights when she would flip on those old soul records, it may have been that the only way she could imagine telling the story was to include herself, and in denying herself that option, she needed to think of a new way to look at the situation. She had to tell the story once in her head so that she could manually erase all the traces of herself.

When my wife talked with these people, she tried never to pass judgment. She tried to bring out parts of their story that she felt were important and that she thought they were avoiding.

My wife laid on the couch and listened to soul to ease her mind, to exempt herself from the stories of the world outside, to allow herself to become what she considered an auditor.

She'd have to let the voice teach itself to her, so she could learn how to speak it.

6.

My wife told me a story once, when we were not yet married, about a man who wore little wire rim glasses framed by long hair and a matching auburn beard.

My wife said this man offered her his story easily outside a general store in some western town.

She'd gone on a road trip by herself for an entire summer. She assumed there wouldn't be many young people driving through Wyoming or South Dakota. She figured people would leave her alone for a while.

My wife loved the sidewalks of the city, but one summer she wanted to leave them behind so she could come back to them.

She wasted time while she took this trip. She lived out of her car and spent large portions of the day leaning against it in parking lots, taking in the dusty sunlight and the families spilling in and out of their vehicles.

One morning sitting on a bench outside of a general store, she was greeted by a friendly mutt. She set her bags down and petted the dog, but soon the man with the wire rim glasses came up behind the dog apologizing.

My wife said it was no problem. She loved dogs and hadn't seen nearly enough of them lately.

The man said he had hitched in the night before.

The man said to my wife, "I'm the kind of man who likes to buy a woman a cup of coffee to get to know her, no expectations. I'm a rambler. I like to meet as many people as I can."

My wife said, "I like coffee." And they were off.

My wife told me, "It became clear quickly I was never going to get this guy's story. I don't think the man lived a day of his life. He spent all his time defining who he was, like it was a possibility. If I told this man's story, it would be about how incorrect his own version was."

My wife told me what this man had said, this rambler:

"I'm the kind of man who likes to live from day to day. I've never had a steady job, and I never intend to have one."

"I'm the kind of man who loves women serially. I meet women and write their name on my hand, to remember. When we say goodbye, I spit on my hand and rub the name off. Off my hand, out of mind."

"I'm the kind of man who likes all sorts of music. I've played with a lot of bands in my travels. I can play any instrument your posse's lookin' for."

"I'm the kind of man who makes instant friends with people. I've never met someone who could resist my charms."

"I'm the kind of man who tells it like it is, no matter who it hurts. I'm chronically honest. I can't help it. I have a keen eye for the truth and I lack the tact to not call it as I see it."

When my wife told me this story, she shook her head, smiling. "He was so far off. He never told me a single true thing. I had never met someone so set on identifying himself with so many different labels. He didn't tell stories; he told me what categories he fit into. When we were done with three or four cups of coffee we walked out of the coffee shop and I petted his dog as I said my farewell. He tried to convince me to let him stay in my car for the night. Obviously I refused. 'I'm the kind of man who takes no for an answer,' he replied. The man and his dog walked a few paces away before he said, 'You think you have something on me. I can tell by that smile. You think you have all the answers. You might fool the others, but you can't fool me.' And he winked like he'd let me in on a secret and sauntered away, his dog loping at his side. I walked back into the diner to talk to the waitress a little while and tell her about what had happened."

My wife told me the waitress said, "Must happen all the time. Some people are unknowable." She'd misunderstood. She thought my wife was saying he was an enigma.

My wife hadn't intended to pay him such a compliment.

My wife had lost to a man obsessed with fitting himself into his own picture frame.

My wife said, "The only story I could tell that afternoon was ultimately about myself."

"Tricky bastard." My wife laughed, defeated.

7.

My wife knew a little French. We went to the south of France for our honeymoon, stayed in Nice, took day trips along the coast, spent only one day in Paris, threw its proportion of French history to the wind.

My wife spoke French to shopkeepers; waiters spoke English to my wife. The French people became exasperated. They kept trying to convince her to speak English. My wife waved off what she thought were their accommodations. "Arretez!" she would say nonchalantly. She would take her time recalling what words she could say to get her meaning across. Her voice slid through this language I was hearing her speak for the first time. My wife enjoyed the waltz of it. She liked the way everyone was trying to adapt to the others' rhythms, like dancing with strangers.

My wife woke early while I slept. It always rains at night in the South of France, or perhaps it rains in the early morning. Either way, there were first-light puddles in the paved-brick streets, the air damp at sunup. For the people who lived there, the drying rainwater was something to watch happen day after day; it was another part of the set-in-cobblestone routine.

My wife plunked through puddles, the water weighing down her pant hems. She bought baguettes she watched being pulled from the oven.

My wife would haggle in broken French with the little old men in the market down the street for tiny bananas, fresh strawberries, bright bouquets of intricate ranunculus.

I would rise to the smell of the rain my wife dragged in. She smelled of sea and slope and narrow streets yawning "Bon matin."

My wife and I drove to gallery after chapel after mansion and remembered laughingly how people warned us of the rudeness of the French.

We climbed to the top of everything, pressed every button, sat on the base of every sculpture before being shagged off. There was age there, cities built into stone, clinging to the sides of mountains with stubborn, arthritic fingers.

My wife touched art and artifacts that had velvet ropes strung before them. She touched objects older than we could imagine. She helped them age a bit more quickly.

In the Musée d'Orsay, on our only day in Paris, my wife whispered. "Hands," she said, "are full of chemicals that cause things to deteriorate quickly. When I was a child on vacation in Dublin we went to see the Book of Kells. It was under glass in a dimly lit room. They told us if we touched it, it would fall apart. They warned us, 'You don't want to deny other people the chance to see this beautiful artifact, do you?' They spoke like fathers protecting their daughters' virginity."

My wife said, "I wanted to crack the glass, let the book feel my hands."

My wife's eyes glowed mischievously.

My wife, her eyes trained on mine, placed one hand on the foot of a plaster cast model of Rodin's *Balzac*.

My wife took one of my hands and placed it on her face. She placed a hand on top of mine.

She shut her eyes, my hand on her cheek, her hand on mine, her other hand on Balzac. "Have you noticed how hands are born wrinkled, where the finger joints have already been bending for months?"

My wife said, "How must we age from handshakes alone?"

She opened her eyes, squinting in the sun. She raised her eyebrows. What did she want me to say?

8.

MY WIFE CLAIMED A CLOSET as her own as soon as we moved into
our apartment.

She was handy and installed a lock. She kept the tiny key on
a chain she wore on her wrist.

I asked my wife what it was she felt she needed to lock away
from me.

My wife said, "The lock is for me, not you."

She said, "I trust you and know you would contain yourself
not to look in the closet if I asked you not to. But I would be
going in there all the time, if there weren't a little something
that made it more difficult."

With a smile, she said, "What's a little uncharted closet on
the map of this apartment? It's other people's stories in there.
They have nothing to do with you or me. We must contain
ourselves, leave those stories to age. When you begin to age
wine you can't open the cask to check on its progress."

She said, "I'll show you the closet. We can look at the shelves,
but this can't be something we do often. Come on, we'll look
now and that will be the end of it."

She unclasped the bracelet from her wrist and fit the key deftly into the lock.

Her hand moved into the closet to pull a string and light a bank of closely spaced shelves I hadn't even known she put up. I wondered where I'd been.

The shallow shelves ran across the back wall of the closet, probably twenty in all, from top to bottom. I believe I remember only the first three shelves being filled. The fourth shelf held only two tapes. She had just begun.

My wife kindly gave permission. "Go ahead. You can look at the labels if you like."

I smiled at my wife. This was exactly what I wanted. I scanned the first few:

Joe, 37, Chicago: No longer that of the Clocks.

Kim, 19, Chicago: White Napkin.

Allan, 72, Chicago: A True Correspondence.

I asked my wife, "Name, age, location and then what? Title?"

"Yes."

"How do you decide the title?" I asked.

"That's the one thing that's mine. The title says something about the way I understand the contents. That's the little liberty I allow myself."

I smiled at my wife again. This was her cue. "Alright, out we go then. I don't want you getting attached."

"Come on, shoo," she said half jokingly, though I could tell she was ready to lock the space away again.

I asked what I had to ask. "Can we listen to some of them?"

My wife pulled the string to darken the closet.

My wife locked the door with the tiny key.

She fastened the bracelet back on her wrist.

"Of course not." She hurried to our bedroom, began changing her clothes for work. "You know better than that."

9.

My wife was the start of me.

If someone were to ask how I had changed since I met her I would be unable to find the words. It wasn't that I changed because of knowing her.

It's more accurate to say that I began.

She was enough for me. She was enough for the both of us.

How we met is inconsequential, but if it must be told: through friends, first in a large group and then slowly spending more and more time together alone.

Sometimes it's difficult for me to remember time we spent with other people. She filled the space. She eclipsed others. She made other people seem less real.

My wife didn't throw a Frisbee onto my blanket on the quad.

My wife didn't ask one of her friends to tell me she liked me.

She didn't send me anonymous love letters and mixed tapes.

Most importantly, she did not ask me to tell her my story.

We met in spring when our groups of friends somehow combined. Her friends told us about her obsession with stories. They told us how she would talk to anyone, how she could get anyone to talk, how she would begin speaking to someone new before the last person had finished their story, but how people seemed comfortable waiting for her.

It's true. When we began talking I didn't think myself special. I assumed she wanted my story as well, not because I was intriguing, but as another name to check off some imagined list.

I wasn't resistant to the effort. I figured if she was as good as they said, my story would come out without my even knowing.

When we had been hanging out for about a week, I thought I had proved them all wrong, as she wasn't pulling my story from me. It turned out I was the one getting it wrong. She didn't try to draw stories from people she planned on keeping around. She wasn't interested in getting me in one go.

This is not to say that my wife was not genuinely interested in the people she got stories from. She was. But from me, she was looking for a lengthier tale. She was seeking a sum which might take a bit longer to add up.

When we spent our first evening alone together it was an accident. A large group of us were supposed to meet and go on a pub-crawl one night, and by the time we were scheduled to leave, only my wife and I had congregated at my apartment. Everyone else had called one by one to send their last-minute regrets. When the last call came in I asked my wife if she still wanted to go, she kicked off her shoes and settled into my mangy couch.

"Let's take it easy." She picked up a magazine on my coffee table. I sat down next to her, but not too close.

We didn't stay up all night talking.

We didn't sleep together.

We didn't even kiss.

We talked for a couple hours and then she went home relatively early. We were both supposed to work in the morning and we were relieved that we didn't have to go out. We didn't talk about deep and personal feelings. We talked about what movies we wanted to see and the good books we had recently read. We gossiped a little about our friends. I didn't take it personally when she wanted to go. I didn't think I was missing out. I wasn't even sure if I was interested in her in any romantic way.

We were just two friends that got ditched by everyone else that night.

Nothing suddenly changed. We kept seeing each other around and eventually we started to go off from the group, just the two of us. We would be at a bar and go play darts, or once we paired up for the rides at a carnival. No, we didn't kiss on the Ferris wheel. We might have slid together playfully on the Tilt-a-whirl, but that was the most that happened.

We moved slowly. Everything felt comfortable. I'd get nervous with her sometimes, but then again, I got nervous with all girls, even ones I knew I had no chance with.

And I would be lying to say that this comfort was not complicated by a certain sense of mystery that seemed to shroud her ever so slightly .

In the beginning I thought it was annoying. I thought she was trying to appear enigmatic. I would ask questions and she wouldn't answer. I assumed she imagined herself a bad girl, with enough secrets to keep people interested without ever letting anyone close.

As we spent more time together, I realized she avoided only the questions she didn't like and that this was some peculiar form of honesty.

When she didn't answer a question it seemed the logical response. I began to wish other people acted the same way.

When we'd known each other a few months, I asked her if she had my story yet.

My wife looked at me surprised. I had never mentioned that I knew about her habit. She said, "Nope. I don't want it. There's a difference between people and their stories."

I asked her what the difference was.

She didn't answer.

That night I thought a lot about what she had told me in that one sentence, and still I wasn't sure what she could mean. I woke up in the middle of the night and everything felt clear, though I couldn't explain it. "There's a difference between people and their stories." I didn't understand why it suddenly worked, but it was the truth.

I called her in the morning. I didn't call any of our friends for the number. I looked her name up in the phone book and luckily she was listed. I called her early, and she answered the phone, groggy and somewhat disoriented. "I understand," I said. "'There's a difference between people and their stories.' I'm sorry I asked what it was last night. I get it now."

She knew exactly what I was talking about even in her sleepy state. "Good. I'm glad to hear that. It takes some people years to figure it out." She yawned. "You're a morning thinker, huh?"

I had no idea what she was talking about again so I asked her to clarify.

"You think your clearest thoughts in the morning, is that right?"

"Oh! No, not at all. I figured it out in the middle of the night. I mulled it over and fell back asleep. I had to call you immediately to let you know. This feels huge. You know?" I was elated to be functioning at what felt was a heightened level of consciousness.

"Yeah, I do. Go back to sleep though. I am anything but a morning thinker. I'll talk to you later, alright?"

"Definitely. Thank you. I'm sorry again about last night. Thank you for not answering. It was definitely worth it to figure it out myself. You know there's that quote, I think Gertrude Stein said it, that one doesn't know something until one's written it themselves—"

"Good. Sleep well, then." I could hear annoyance, with what I hoped were traces of amusement, in her voice, but how I had wanted to talk to her about this event! I had been sure I would call and she would be astounded that someone had finally gotten it. I thought then would be the time where we talked for hours over the phone and then decided that we needed to meet in person. Everything felt like it had been building up to that moment, and then she had written it off to be something simple and not nearly as significant as I had imagined it.

I hung up the phone and laid back down on the top of my sheets. It was that morning after she had apparently snubbed one of my questions that I realized how valuable she was to me.

I became more aggressive then. I called her more often to see if she wanted to spend time together. I sent her flowers. I visited her at the restaurant where she worked and left her a generous tip and a card.

It wasn't long before she stopped returning my calls, before she refused the flowers I sent, before she asked her manager to seat me in any section but hers.

She didn't come to any functions she thought I might attend, which was anything either of our friends planned. I never turned down an invitation in the hopes I might run into her and apologize for my overzealous behavior.

After having not seen her for about a month, I stopped attending any gatherings at all. I went to class. I went to work. I went home. I became a sorry case of a man. I grew a beard that I failed to trim regularly. I stopped making myself real dinners and ate horrible food out of cans. I didn't read. I got the rabbit-ear antenna out of the closet, hooked it to the television I had only used to watch movies.

About a month later a cousin of mine was in a play and I promised her I would go see it. I arrived late, missing the first scene and getting seated in a random open seat near the back. At intermission I didn't try and find my real seat. I was exhausted from the effort of being in public.

After the show, I was one of the first to exit the auditorium, and I waited to greet my cousin in the lobby.

I felt a tap on my shoulder, and turned, expecting to see my cousin.

There was my wife. I could say nothing, just stared, astonished that she was there.

She smiled, genuine and concerned. "Still got it all figured out there, buddy?" I must have looked awful. She could see my state of turmoil. I know I was unkempt. And still, there was a sense that her fist was being held up: the champion of a TKO. Her face moved quickly between smug and apprehensive.

Of course, I had imagined this happening a million times. I had planned exactly what I was going to say, but I had never imagined she would say something first.

"I like the beard." She said, tugging near my chin ever so gently.

Was it possible that she had no idea how greatly she had devastated me, by not returning my calls, by avoiding me at all costs? Surely our friends had informed her of the state I was in. Surely someone had let it slip how obsessed I'd become, how much the idea of her had come to mean to me, that she wasn't simply another crush.

"Are you here alone?" she asked, unthrown by how unresponsive I was. She squinted her eyes at me now, and tilted her head, unsure what the problem was. "I'm sorry about not returning your calls. I don't deal well with people acting aggressively. Usually I'm the one who figures out a situation and takes it forward. You caught me off guard, pal."

I was utterly perplexed. She was whispering in my ear, using words like *buddy* and *pal*. I had been sure she was the one a month before; I had been sure she was the one the *night* before. I'd been sure I had messed up the best thing that had ever happened to me. I had regressed so far as to think of my loss in those awful terms: "the one that got away" and "the love of my life." Right then I hated her a little bit. Why did she get to be calm enough to call me *pal?*

I tried to look through her, searched the space beyond her for some sort of answer, and then my cousin emerged from the theater, and threw her arms around me.

My wife winked and waved, walked out.

My cousin hugged me, and my arms, wrapped around her, felt foreign. Her hair was kinky from pin curls that had been hidden under a wig. Her face was pale, scrubbed of the heavy greasepaint. Her back felt damp with sweat. I didn't enjoy hugging her. I waited for her to loosen her grip.

I said, "Congratulations."

I said, "You were wonderful."

I said, "I never knew you were so talented."

"Was it worth coming out of your little hole?" my cousin asked.

She loosened her grip and I held her at arms length. "Absolutely." I kissed her forehead and we walked to the nearest diner to get a cup of coffee and a piece of pie, to talk about the show. Something felt full again. Something felt started over.

The next day my wife called and asked if I wanted to meet her somewhere for lunch. I agreed immediately. I shaved my beard that morning. It was summer now and I was slightly paler where the beard had been.

At lunch my wife told me how she had missed me.

She told me how her stories had been huge since she met me. She told me she thought she might have begun to bridge the gap between people's stories and themselves.

I told her I wasn't sure what she meant and she smiled, happy to hear this. "I think you and I could work together."

I was wary to start anything, but also becoming excited again. "Work together?"

"I think you and I should maybe start dating. I'll make lots of vague statements and if you figure out what they mean in the middle of the night, you're never allowed to tell me again." She winked and I knew she must have known how I had suffered in want of her. "I'm not a puzzle to be figured out, and I think if you figure something out, it's probably just for you, and probably has nothing to do with me. Deal?"

I nodded, terrified to answer the wrong way.

We began seeing each other exclusively then. We moved in after six months. We were engaged in a year. We were married six months after that, and then she was gone ten years later.

It's been five years now.

I'm cooking full meals.

My face is clean-shaven.

The day I realized my wife was gone, our apartment was ransacked, torn apart. Almost all of it was emptied onto the floor and pulled into pieces.

The day I realized my wife was gone, everything else went with her.

And I tried to bring it back, but it never came, so I relented.

And now I've carried on.

10.

MY WIFE SAID, "I like to think about how our bodies constantly make themselves. How we keep ourselves alive." She enjoyed studying the mechanical workings of the body.

My wife attributed this interest to an experiment she did in her high school biology class.

In this experiment they penned in the outline of a square inch on their hands. They then took a hot probe and poked random places within the square. In black ink they marked with a tiny dot the places where the heat of the probe was distinguishable. The number of places within this square inch that the hand actually registered heat from the probe was quite small. They did the same experiment in the same square with a frozen probe. About an equal number of spots, different ones, felt the cold probe. They marked these areas with tiny red dots.

These dots indicated temperature nerve endings present at the surface of the skin, and their absence indicated places where the skin was not sensitive to temperature.

"Every inch of the human body," my wife said, "is blind to something."

"He was a terrible teacher," she added, "except for that experiment. That experiment changed my life."

My wife said, "People think the brain continues out into the universe, but it doesn't. It ends at your skin. If you want to change your life, change your body. I'm not talking just form or appearance, but any physical dislocation; moving somewhere else changes your body, because you're situated in a different context."

I smiled. It was hard to keep up all the time, but I did my best. In the years we'd been together, I'd learned that's what she wanted. She slapped my arm. "I'm serious. This is important. You can laugh, but in the end, our bodies are where we reside for our whole lives."

Soon after, on a cold day, walking home from the grocery store, my wife suddenly stopped. "Breathe in," she commanded. I did, eager to placate her so we might get home. "Now, quickly, breathe out."

"Do it again," she said, "and this time, feel the temperature."

"I was breathing before you told me how," I countered.

"Don't be a smartass. This is remarkable."

I breathed in and out a few more times. "Cold in and hot out. What's your point?"

"See how quickly you did that? The air out here must be thirty degrees. When you exhale, feel the warmth in your mouth? In seconds, you've heated that air almost seventy degrees. Isn't that incredible?"

I'd never thought of it that way, so I nodded. Genuinely.

"Every one of those molecules of oxygen and carbon dioxide touched your blood. Every minute of the day we bathe ourselves in blood. Every cell of our bodies is touched by our blood. And we can feel it happen. Put a finger to your wrist or neck, or lie back and you can feel blood beat through your stomach. We're flooding ourselves constantly. No wonder the air we breathe out is warm. It's gone everywhere there is to go."

Eyes wide, my wife looked like she'd arrived at her conclusion ahead of time.

With the hand free of groceries she tugged my sleeve, asking for a response.

"What made you think of that?" I asked.

"I was walking and I keyed into the temperature of my breath and suddenly came the revelation: everything our bodies do constantly, how capable we are of the extraordinary, even something like heating air *really* quickly."

"You're right. In those terms, blood becomes a sort of a romantic notion, this entity, the most familiar resident of our bodies, huh? And our breath, then, because it's ridden through the blood, flowed through our bodies, becomes an intimate thing. Pretty wonderful," I said. "Magnificent."

"It is, isn't it?" She nodded, satisfied, her thoughts wandering further.

We began to walk again, laughing as we exhaled white clouds and walked through them, breaking relics of our respiration with our faces.

11.

MY WIFE MET A LITTLE boy in a sandbox. He was building castles.

She had been out for a walk through the park. It was the beginning of fall and the leaves were just starting to change.

My wife had gone on the walk for lime, for tangerine and lemon.

My wife had gone on the walk for all the citrus colors of the autumn leaves, before they burnt through to brown, when their death still smelled fresh, didn't crinkle underfoot.

The little boy in the sandbox wore a knit cap pulled down over his ears.

My wife was fascinated by his aloneness. There was no one else at the playground.

My wife watched him with great interest as she walked. She wasn't watching the cracks in the sidewalk and her eyes stayed on the boy when her hands hit the ground.

My wife hobbled over to the sandbox, plunked down on the edge to get a better look at her scraped knee.

The little boy said hello to her.

The little boy told my wife he was eight and a half.

He told her he didn't go to school today.

He told her he liked her scrape.

He asked if it was real.

He had not seen my wife fall.

The boy told my wife sometimes he drew on himself with red ink to make it look like he had been hurt.

He told my wife he had watched a program on special effects makeup where people drew and glued things on themselves for a living.

He told her that now he knew what he wanted to do.

My wife told the boy that, yes, the cut was real.

She told him one day he wouldn't want to pretend to be hurt; he would spend all his times of well-being remembering away the hurt.

The boy told my wife, "Your cut hurts."

My wife confirmed his statement with a nod.

He said, "Aren't you going to ask why I'm not in school?"

My wife shook her head. She smiled at him, silently telling him to go ahead.

"My mom won't come downstairs. I bring her breakfast in the morning and leave. I come home and my dad makes us dinner. We bring the food upstairs and eat together sitting on her bed. Today I didn't go. I took my backpack and I walked here instead of school. My dad said today was going to be the last warm day and I wanted to build one last castle before it was too cold."

My wife stared, listening.

The boy looked down at his castle. "My mom's not sick. She doesn't cough or throw up. She just won't come downstairs. I think she will someday, but I don't know when. I thought it would be okay if I missed a day of school to build one last castle before winter. Now I'm worried they might have called my mom. If they did call, she would be worried. Maybe she would come downstairs. I would go home to check, but if they didn't call, I don't want to get in trouble. If they did call, I don't want her to go back upstairs. My mom's not sick, though. She just won't come down."

"I think you should go home."

"Is that what you're supposed to say, or something you want to say?"

"Sometimes it's hard to tell."

"I like your pearls. My nana wears pearls like yours."

"Thank you. I wish I were your nana," my wife said.

The little boy asked, "Why?"

For this child, who was giving so much, my wife broke her own rules. It was a rare instance, where she realized how valuable it could be to give a little back. "I'm still waiting to feel grown-up. I think being a grandmother would be a sure sign."

He wrinkled his nose at her. "You're grown-up. How old are you, thirty-one and half?"

My wife thought for a minute. Her eyes widened. "Thirty-one and a half today exactly. How did you know?"

"I'm good with age."

My wife took charge of the situation as she did so well. My wife did the appropriate thing that afternoon for the little boy and then she came home. I was sitting in a large armchair, going over some notes for a lecture . We'd moved in together about six months prior. I was getting comfortable being the one my wife came home to.

She laid down on our patched leather couch. "When I was a child..." my wife began.

"You spoke as I child?" I tried to finish her sentence with a joke, smirking at how clever I was. I expected to hear a giggle, but when I didn't, I looked over at her.

Her eyes were wet.

"I'm sorry. Go on." I hadn't realized.

My wife began again. "When I was a child, I was frightened of the elderly. I would avoid them at all costs. I remember hating to visit my grandmother because of the smell of her house, because she would force me to take home spiral notebooks that had solid-colored covers, rather than the ones I eyed at drugstores covered in pictures of kittens. I disliked the way the ice cubes she pulled from the tray for my sodas were shrunken small and wilted with age because she never used them herself; the ice irritated her teeth. My mother and I visited my grandmother every Thursday morning in the summer."

My wife said, "We would pick her up from the beauty shop where she had her hair done and take her to breakfast."

She said, "We would take her grocery shopping."

She said, "We would take her to the bank, and then to the dollar store."

My wife said, "We would go back to her house, and my mother and grandmother would have tea. My grandma'd get a glass coated with a thin layer of dust, crack two or three emaciated ice cubes into the cup and pop a can of cream soda for me. We would sit at her kitchen table with the curtains drawn and the overhead light dim with too few bulbs. I would draw windows and people with flat skulls on scrap paper with pens pulled from the floral centerpiece while my mother and grandmother settled bills on the plastic tablecloth, the macramé place mats. Framed formations of sunflower seeds hung on the wall above my head.

"I'd listen to them. and predict how much longer we were going to have to stay by what topic they had moved onto.

"If it was who had visited my grandmother in the past week it would be at least another hour.

"If it was who had died recently, maybe forty-five minutes.

"If it was a new disease my grandmother had read about in the newspaper and now believed she had, we were in the last half hour.

"When we moved on to a list of errands my grandmother needed my mom to run for her in the next week before we would visit again, we had about fifteen minutes.

"When my grandmother started talking about how she had lived too long without my grandfather, how she was ready to go up and join him, how death would be better than living like this, we were bound to leave the kitchen any minute, kissing my grandmother on the head, letting her cry alone.

"As I got older, I started visiting my grandmother on my own. I didn't like her attitude, but I was fascinated and decided it would be my mission to figure out what happened to her, why she felt the need to end each experience by telling us she wanted to die."

My wife sat silent for a long time. I knew better than to prompt her. She would continue when she was ready. She would stop only if she couldn't say any more.

My wife said, "Each ending felt like a tease to her. Each goodbye felt not final enough. After eighty-five years of farewells, she grew unsatisfied with their outcome; their purpose seemed superfluous. She felt the need to make them something she used to get her hopes up, to remind us that maybe that would be the last time we had to perform the ritual of kissing her forehead, leaving her to cry alone in the kitchen."

My wife didn't cry.

"I want to be old. I want to watch myself age. I'm uncomfortable being young. I want to forget what it was like to be a child."

My wife said, "I met a little boy who built sandcastles for a living today. He was young. Youth isn't wasted on children. It's inflicted on them, when they can't tell what's hit them."

I worried about my wife. I asked, "Shall we mark our heights against the wall?"

She nodded solemnly. This was something we had learned to do together. On bad days we would make the other stand up as straight as possible against a thin piece of molding that ran along the bathroom door. We would take a pen and mark how tall we were that day. The divots where our heights hadn't changed since we met were a constant. We could look at those deepening furrows of measurement and sigh that we hadn't shrunk, that we weren't slowly becoming gigantic. Our size was something even and clear, unchanged by a difficult day. My wife knew days like this gave her the age she desired, but she liked the idea that they couldn't touch her height.

She and I were tall: five foot eleven and six foot four, respectively. We were *tall*, and we often spoke of how this meant so much.

We had learned to appreciate that people had to look up at us even if they didn't look up to us. We had been raised to feel awkward when standing straight and we had been raised reaching for the top shelf our grandmothers couldn't quite get to. Tall was our way. We changed light bulbs and bent our knees in group pictures.

12.

LATER IN OUR TIME TOGETHER, my wife would wake in the night.

She wasn't a light sleeper, but there was one sound that could stir her without fail.

When it was warm out, we left the windows open. If it was quiet and if the traffic was slow, we could hear the faint sound of a tin sign swaying down the street.

The sign was lightweight. It didn't take more than the slightest breeze or a car driving by to start it swinging.

I could sleep right through the sound, but I know my wife would wake often because of it.

I could play music loudly and she wouldn't so much as twitch. But at night, in the warm silence, she would wake to the cool squeak of that sign below.

She knew there was no use tossing and turning. She couldn't try to ignore it. Closing the window wouldn't even be enough.

She would simply stand quietly from her side of the bed, open the bedroom door and pad to the kitchen where she would flip on the light and lean against the counter, arms folded patiently, waiting for the breeze to subside.

I would wake and find her side of the bed empty.

I'd stumble into the kitchen blindly and stand in front of her. My sleep-swollen hands would find their way to her hair and as my fingers began to thread through the soft tangle on her head, her eyes would shut and her chin would lift and she would bask in the light of the overhead lamp like it was the warmest of summer afternoons.

Eventually she would lift her arms in a stretch, yawning, like a cat in a spot of sun, and then she'd place her hands on my shoulders to still me. Her lips would form the shape of a "sh" but no sound would come out and I would watch her listen, afraid to breathe, afraid to blink.

The sign had silenced itself.

Her hands would slide down my shoulders, down my chest and abdomen, onto my hips and she would push me gently away so she could walk back to our bedroom and climb into bed. Her hand would hit the light switch on her way out of the kitchen, a moment before it might seem like an afterthought.

I would stand in darkness for a few seconds and listen to the rumple of the linens as she climbed into bed. Then I would run the faucet, letting the water get cold, as I pulled a glass from the cupboard. While downing the glassful in a gulp with my right hand, my left hand would tap the faucet off with measured accuracy. I would set the glass in the sink and count the steps back to the bedroom where I would find my wife already fast asleep.

13.

AFTER RECORDING A STORY each night for three years, my wife stopped. I think the hiatus lasted about six months.

It wasn't that she told me the stories had ended. I knew because I stopped waiting for her to come out of closed-door rooms.

She didn't have a ritual place to tell her stories; she brought her tape recorder into whatever room I wasn't in at the moment.

I would have to wait for her to finish before I could enter that room, or she would need to stop and start over.

My wife never told me when she was about to tell a story. It was an unspoken thing. She would disappear behind a door and I would hear the faint stirrings of her narrating a tale, but I would never try to listen.

It would be a lie if I didn't occasionally catch a word or a phrase, but I directed my attention to anything beside her voice. I was nervous I'd hear something I wasn't supposed to and bring it up later by accident. I knew my wife would share with me what she wanted, in a room where the doors were open.

For about six months though, she never disappeared to speak to the containment of a shut-off room and a rewound cassette tape, and I knew this because she shut down.

My wife would come home from work, lie on the couch and play folk music instead of her usual soul records.

I heard females wailing Cuban revolution songs.

I heard the twang of steel strings being plucked.

I heard lyrics about the rape of the land and the earthy smell of desire.

Because of this soundtrack, I was on edge.

About a month into this hiatus, I sat at the foot of the couch where my wife slid her feet up to accommodate me.

My wife looked at me expectantly and I forgot everything I had planned to say. My wife had the power to make me forget: a bittersweet fact, for when I needed most to forget, she was gone.

She looked away, settling her eyes back to space, her ears back to listening, assuming I had just wanted to be near her.

She still had the power to call up a knot of silence in me, when all I wanted were the meticulous strings of words I had composed. So I improvised, inadequately, saying, "No stories, huh?"

"No."

"Haven't felt like it?"

"I need to stop for a while." She looked up at me again, this time with blankness, an innocent emptiness I found somewhat frightening.

I narrowed my brow. "Everything alright?"

As I said this, I became nauseous with its inadequacy.

She shrugged.

"What is it?" I put a hand on her foot and she flinched.

"I feel too full right now. I'm overwhelmed... I'm not sure why exactly, but I figure it can't hurt to pare everything down a bit. To live a bit more simply for a while."

"Is it the stories?" She never talked much about them. I didn't want to pry. I knew they were her own and they had nothing to do with me.

"Might be," she said, shrugging again. It was out of character for her to be so indifferent. It unnerved me. "I talked to a butcher last week. I met an old college friend for a late lunch on the south side and she told me I had to go to this butcher in the area. It was some of the best meat she'd ever eaten and she said I should go and get some high-quality filets, as a treat for you and me. I wandered to the address she told me after our lunch, thinking I would give it a try while I was down there. I spotted the sign for the shop about three storefronts away and, of course, I didn't notice a fire hydrant and I tripped and by the time I'd gathered myself up again, and reached the store, the butcher was flipping the CLOSED sign in the window. I gave him a pleading look, certain he would be happy to have one last customer for the day.

"I was entirely wrong. He looked at me sternly, almost grimaced, and sliced the air with the knife edge of one fat hand." She demonstrated this, karate-chopping the empty space above her reclining figure. "He didn't make a single gesture of apology, just retreated behind the counter and began closing up in a leisurely fashion. He didn't appear to be in a rush to get anywhere."

My wife said, "I watched him carry trays of meat to the coolers in the backroom."

My wife said, "I watched him wipe the counters down."

She said, "I watched him shut the lights off: the ones in the coolers, the fluorescents overhead.

"I stood outside and watched until he pulled his coat from a hook on the wall inside the backroom. He headed toward the front door and only then did he notice I was still there. He looked at me confusedly and unlocked the door to let himself out. He opened the door and began, 'I'm sorry. You'll have to come back tomorrow. We are closed for the day.'

"He began to walk away from the store, from me. I asked him, 'Why wouldn't you let in one more customer?'

"'You think you're so important I should change my routine for you? I close every day at 5:00, whether there is someone on his way or not. If I let you in, I should let in the fellow down the block as well, the fellow stuck on a stalled train? Where do you think I should draw the line?'

"He kept walking and I stopped following him. Usually I would have chased him down, but I didn't. I was exhausted. I can't remember someone ever being so reluctant to talk to me."

My wife said, "I stopped."

She said, " I watched him disappear around a corner."

She said, "I regretted him even before the corner carried him away."

My wife's face looked lost. "These stories are how I've relied on myself; they're what I expect of myself. When I failed, I wasn't sure what to do. I felt like a lost lamb, and I was my own shepherd: all I need to do was gather a few stories to pull myself back in, but I'm not sure I should. I started thinking about what or who I was without them. I realized I know myself differently than anyone else knows me, than even *you* know me. I wondered if this was alright. I don't know yet, so I'm taking a break from the stories. I'm absenting myself from the antique stores. I've left the key to the closet in my sock drawer in hopes I'll think about it less. They're just other people's histories. I need to start thinking a bit larger. I'm pretty sure it's this proximity I find too stifling." She sat up, swung her feet off the couch, down to the floor, stared straight ahead, "Don't say anything right now, okay? I know you might think the idea of stopping the stories altogether is either a good or a bad idea, but don't say which. Or maybe you think I'm being absurd and blowing all of this out of proportion. But I don't

want to resent you either way in the future. I want to figure this
out on my own, for myself. Deal?"

I had understood this habit of collecting stories as some sort
of necessary obsession. It was a quirk I knew about, and loved,
and was afraid to examine out of existence. I loved her with
or without these stories lurking in the closet, but the fact that
she was compelled to do such a thing had certainly been a large
part of why I had grown so attached to her. I said, "Fine. The
decision is, of course, entirely yours."

I looked away, not trying to pressure a reply. Our sightlines
ran parallel to each other, landed on the painting covering the
opposite wall. It had been given to us as a wedding gift.

The picture was almost cartoonish, looked like an old
promotional poster for some sort of French nightclub. A woman
in a pouf of a silver dress stood pulling the hand of a stubborn
seated man, dressed in an ill-fitting tuxedo. The faces of these
two figures were what made the painting so intriguing. The
woman had a look of utter surprise on her face, mouth open,
eyes wide, as if she had been caught trying to take the man
away. The man looked blissful, seemingly certain that he wanted
nothing more in life than to have her pulling his hand.

My wife shut her eyes and said, "Thank you."

14.

AROUND THIS TIME, MY WIFE started throwing irrelevant elements into arguments.

She had impeccable logic most of the time, but she knew exactly how to win a fight with me. If she avoided logic and went on tangents that were completely unrelated to the point I was trying to make, she would win because I would get confused and sidetracked.

Our bathroom sink was clogged. My wife left me a note asking me to work on it when I woke up. She would be back around noon.

When she returned home I had emptied the contents of the cabinet beneath the sink into the kitchen and I was on the phone with a plumber. My wife looked around, astonished, wondering why all of this stuff was everywhere.

I told my wife that while I was snaking the drain, a portion of the pipe had rotted out and I poked a hole through it. My wife looked horrified already. Her eyes were wild and her mouth agape. I told her the plumber would be unable to come until Monday because his truck was in the shop. My wife said, "You're kidding."

I shook my head. She went off on me in a completely unexpected way: "Did you happen to see how clean that cabinet was?"

I looked at my wife, confused.

She shouted, "I reorganized that cabinet a week ago!"

I told her I was sorry but I'd had to get to the pipe.

"Yeah, but you can't say that cabinet wasn't *clean*!"

At this point I chuckled a little, because I had no idea what she was getting at. I said, "Yes, the cabinet was indeed quite clean."

"See?"

I claimed that I did see because I sensed if I let this go, we might move on and not talk any more about this accident that was no one's fault, just a matter of poor timing. We were supposed to have a dinner party that evening.

We set about finding places to stash the bins of toiletries in closets and under our bed. My wife said, "I should cancel the party."

"Don't be silly. We'll put some hand sanitizer in the bathroom and redirect them to the kitchen sink. It's not like one room's far from the other."

My wife was conceding, letting the drama go, when she moved a bottle of bleach from the kitchen table. Beneath the bottle, on her good red tablecloth, was a wet spot faded to pink. My wife pitched the bottle into the basket. My wife shouted, "Why can you never not ruin something?"

"Excuse me?"

"You ruin everything. You are never not ruining something."

I stood, bewildered, watching my wife rip the cloth off our kitchen table. "My wife is logical," I kept telling myself. I knew I didn't ruin everything. She had used a double negative; this was proof she wasn't thinking. My wife spent her free time ruining, or as she liked to call it, *aging* her clothes on purpose.

I said, "You know I don't ruin things on purpose. I put a bottle on the table and it leaked. It's hardly like I meant to do it."

She knew I was right, but she went on to vent. "No! You are always ruining something." This time she sounded less enthused by her anger. She had corrected her grammar. She was calming down. "What if I ruined your favorite shirt?"

I unwisely laughed again, and she pushed my shoulder almost playfully, hiding behind a grimace. I said, "Since when do I have favorite articles of clothing?"

"That's what I mean. I can never get even with you because you are inhumanly unattached to everything."

I shrugged. "So if I had a favorite shirt, you would ruin it to get back at me?"

She lifted her chin into the air. I was a few inches taller than her, so when she wanted to appear haughty and superior, it often seemed like an exaggeration of her looking up at me. She said, "No. I wouldn't have ruined your favorite shirt, because I love you and people who love each other don't ruin each other's stuff." She raised her eyebrows as if the comment was a trump card. She turned with the basket of cleaning supplies and began attempting to cram them into the cabinet below the kitchen sink instead.

After we cleaned up, she collapsed onto our bed.

I pulled the door shut and watched some special on the domestication of feral cats on PBS.

When she emerged she was heading to the bathroom to shower before the party. I asked if she was feeling better, hoping she had cooled off a bit.

"You'll never get it, will you?" she asked. I didn't worry myself too much about her response. I wrote it off as another irrelevancy and turned back to the television.

I heard her turn the water on, a white noise rush like an erased cassette tape.

15.

WHEN THE STORIES STOPPED, my wife started smoking again. My wife sat on the windowsill to the fire escape rather than the couch.

It had been ages since she smoked.

I knew I was supposed to be angry that she was doing something so bad for her health.

I knew I was supposed to look at her perched on the windowsill half-in half-out of the apartment with disdain for the cancerous scent she was exhaling all over our home, into the cool night air. I knew I should think it was ridiculous that she opened a window so widely, multiple times a day in December when the snow was beginning to accumulate.

I was supposed to be even more disgusted by this in the morning.

But I wasn't. I liked the way she looked.

I liked the broad inflations of her chest on the inhale.

I liked the collapse of her shoulders, heavy with all that weight, on the exhale.

I liked the delicate poise of her hand, wrist balanced on a bent knee, the limp bend of her fingers.

I liked the contrast of the white smoke to the night sky and I liked the silhouette of her form against the morning sun.

I liked the flick of her thumb on the lighter, the Popeye grimace with which she sucked in the first gulp of air.

I liked the little slivers of cellophane I found glinting around on the carpet.

I liked the ashy flavor of her.

Her mouth tasted of urns and volcanoes.

I liked the butts I found in the cheap ashtray we kept for smoking guests and the rings of her bright lipstick decorating the filtered ends.

I know I shouldn't have, but I supported her. When she put Marlboro Lights on the grocery list, I asked for them from the cashier without moral hesitation.

When the clerks asked if I wanted them in the bag or with me, I held out my hand and pocketed them so that I might hand them to my wife personally.

I pocketed them so that I might receive some of her gratitude immediately, a kiss on the cheek, as she pulled the loose end of the cellophane and unwrapped the package, eager for the soothing relief.

After she took her first drag, I kissed her mouth, in love and happy to help.

16.

I ASKED THE QUESTION, sure of the answer, but my wife said, "Deaf." I was certain she'd rather be blind.

"Really?" I asked, confused. Maybe she was being contrary.

The question surfaced after we had seen a woman in the art museum with her seeing eye dog. We wondered how and why a blind person would go to an art museum, whether they might be allowed special privileges or something, like running their hands over the statues. We wondered whether there were floor plans printed in Braille. We were on a schedule, though, and we were polite, so we didn't follow her around to figure out what was happening.

In the gift shop at the end of the day we saw the woman flipping through a row of art calendars priced at half-off because it was already the middle of January. Her dog was seated contentedly at her feet.

"She must be only partially blind," my wife said.

"Or maybe she just wanted to bring her dog to the museum," I replied, in good humor.

My wife seemed to consider this for a moment before moving on. We paid for a handful of postcards and an art book. On our way out the huge glass doors I asked the question.

I heard my wife's answer and distrusted it.

"But you listen to your records every night. You record stories on cassette tapes instead of writing them down. You're saying that if tomorrow you had to choose between being blind or deaf, you would be deaf? I don't believe it for a second."

She sighed. "The situation is ridiculous in and of itself. I'm never going to be given that choice. If either of those unfortunate events should occur, I would, of course, learn to deal with it, but if I had to choose right this moment, especially after that afternoon we just spent *seeing* beauty, I would say I would rather be deaf. I don't care if I ever listen to those tapes again. I would rather spend my time gathering more stories than being nostalgic for the past or listening to them and thinking about what a wonderful storyteller I am."

"But, why, then, do you record the stories at all?"

"For the sake of time. They need to go somewhere. I need somewhere to store them so I can start over again."

"What does that mean?"

My wife stopped walking. The sidewalk was crowded. People bumped into us. My wife looked at me like I had offended her deeply.

"Well, come on!" I said. "That was *so* cryptic. You can't say something like that and expect me to roll with it. Did that mean anything? Did you want to avoid answering my question?"

My wife was furious. "Let's hear *your* answer to the question. Would you rather be blind or deaf?"

"Deaf, but I don't focus my life around listening to people's stories, and recording them on cassette tapes!"

My wife's expression shifted to one of triumph, "You're right about that. You most certainly do not listen. I'm sure it would be quite easy for you to give that up. I'm not saying I want to be deaf. You made me choose; I chose. You can't tell me my choice is not my choice. It's mine. Does it drive you crazy that you have no control over that?" My wife broke through the crowd of people passing us, to get to the staircase leading down to the el station.

I stood for a moment, watching her, astonished. When my wife had disappeared out of my sight, I started after her, pushing through the sidewalk traffic. I tried to race down the stairs, but I got caught behind a slow, elderly woman. By the time I had scanned my card, I heard a train pulling up and raced toward the track down another staircase. As I arrived on the platform, the train was already pulling away.

My wife was gone.

17.

THIS WAS THE YEAR MY wife had a wall of calendars.

The fourth wall of our bedroom was covered in them. There was no furniture up against this wall, calendars from floor to ceiling.

The wall was not decorated with wall calendars alone, there were day planners affixed to the wall and clipped open day-by-day calendars, and a couple of those vast grid calendars businesses make for some unknown reason. There were even some of those little card calendars that have only the number of the days, almost too small to see printed in little squares of the months.

This wall was one of my wife's rituals. It was another system that helped her make the transfer from day to day. They helped her make it between days when the stories were stalled.

I rarely saw my wife marking the days, but when I did, it was like watching a dance.

She began at the left side of the wall. She had a small stepping stool. The calendars reached to the ceiling, so she had to stand on the stool to reach the highest ones. She took a permanent marker and put an X through the previous day. If today was Monday, she marked off Sunday. She only ever marked off the day she had just woken from.

She made precise and weighty Xs through the days.

If she knew I was watching, she silenced me with the palm of one of her hands flattened in the air as she tore off the page of a day-by-day calendar.

She Xed out horizontally wide days in the day planners.

My wife made delicate tiny Xs through the small cards' numbers.

My wife would work her way down the wall, kneeling on the floor to X out the calendars lowest to the ground. Then she would scoot her stool over a few feet and climb to begin at the ceiling again.

When she was done she would cap her marker. She'd take the time to read the new day's day-by-day information. She had a word-of-the-day calendar. She had some cartoon calendar. She had a calendar providing a random fact each day.

On the days when I watched my wife perform this ritual of marking out the passing of another day, she would share something with me.

She would read me a particularly unusual definition.

She would sit down beside me and show me the punch line of the cartoon.

She would say, "Can you believe this?"

I would raise my eyebrows with surprise, smile and laugh as she threw the slips of paper away.

Most days she slept later than I did, but on the odd weekend morning when I stayed in bed, I enjoyed watching her dance against the wall, up and down her one-stepped stepping stool, boosting her already long body to the ceiling, arm extended with a marker poised to cross out our days.

18.

THE STORY THAT INEVITABLY BROUGHT my wife out of her funk was that of another local business owner.

My wife, thrilled at the end of her dry-spell, bombarded me when I walked in the door at the end of the day.

"I found a story!" she said while flinging her arms about my neck. She showered my face with wide-spread smiling kisses. She pushed me against the door with a tackling hug and my laptop bag fell to the ground with a blunt thump.

My wife didn't notice.

She placed my hand on her waist.

My wife grasped my shoulder.

My wife pulled our other hands together and projected them away from us, tugging tango-like into the living room, me tripping over my feet, she gliding, for once graceful.

"I ended up talking with the owner of the bakery down the street for almost an hour as he closed the store down for the day. He was a delightful man. You would not believe what he's been through!" She gripped my hand tighter. "You can't imagine how excited I am!" She was still guiding me around the room with our joined fists.

"I think I have a vague idea," I said, laughingly as she twirled on the end of my hand. I, despite all, was still thinking about my dropped laptop lying by the front door.

My wife spun herself into me. "Finally!" She let out a dramatic sigh and collapsed in my arms, forcing me to dip her, to support all of her weight but the little left on the tips of her toes, dragging on the ground.

I carried my wife to the couch. "Let me get this straight. You lost your stories with a butcher. You found them with a baker. If my powers of prediction are all they're cracked up to be—"

She came to life again, eyes wide, warning me. "Don't even say it."

I kissed my wife and she pushed me away playfully. I said, "You knew you had it coming. Anyone would have made the connection. You could have tweaked that story so it didn't sound quite so ridiculous."

My wife stood, haughty now. "I happen to think it's horrifically coincidental that I had to resume my storytelling with a baker, but, as you know, I never 'tweak' a story, even if it means I'm going to have to deal with your ridicule."

I held out my arms, apologizing but triumphant, and my wife collapsed onto the couch so that I might hug her, congratulate her again.

I was relieved. It had been a difficult six months of unpredictable temperaments and a certain sense of ennui that cut through even the most enlivening events. I had spent those months trying to think up ways to break the mood and nothing had worked. It had been all shrugging and sighing.

I was nothing but relieved my wife would begin recording her stories again, and yet what I said was: "I'm going to miss you when you retreat to your shut-in time. I've enjoyed having you for a bit more of each day."

My wife pulled away. Her face, a moment ago spread so wide,

closed in on itself. "I was miserable, and you say you'll miss me when I'm doing what makes me happy, what keeps me sane?"

I told my wife, "I'm so happy your stories have returned."

I told her, "I though it would be romantic to say I would miss you now."

I said, "I *need* the you in my life that tells those stories."

My wife believed me, but she still frowned.

My wife said, "I wouldn't exist."

My wife said, "I'm younger for these quiet months of mine."

She said, "I think it's time to start tacking on the memories again."

The trees were beginning to unravel green in the early April light.

19.

MY WIFE HAD A KEEN ear for chit chat and bullshit, which she claimed were the same thing, and neither of which she cared for.

She wasn't keen to answer questions she didn't have to. There were days I would ask her how she was and it wasn't that she ignored me so much as just didn't feel like answering my question, or saying so. My wife knew the difference between an honest question and a fill-in-the-blank.

My wife knew I cared, but she also knew that I would ask questions like how her day was before I was ready to listen. My wife was honest and forthright, but only when she could tell that the questioners were genuinely curious for an answer. She read people impeccably and so if she could tell someone was asking a question for politeness's sake, she would often not answer, throwing all notions of courtesy out the window.

She could detect even the whitest lies with great ease as well and she had no problem bringing the error to the attention of all involved in the conversation. Often people were astonished at my wife's capacity to notice even the slightest alteration of a story.

My wife was, for the most part, uninterested in making the stories she collected more audience-friendly. She wanted the truth, not the entertainment. My wife thought people who catered their stories to their audience preposterous. She was amazed at how people sought to impress *insignificant her* with a silly story.

My wife paid attention to the way people spoke.

Even if she had never met a person before, a few moments of speaking with them gave her all the information she needed to know. It was in these encounters that her little talent proved the most disconcerting, both because of how easily my wife caught on and also how often it seemed people tweaked information in the first strains of conversation. Everything is a bit altered in the hopes that this person might appear at his most attractive and desirable. Everyone wants to continue talking.

My wife would point out every glitch.

My wife would raise one of her infamously skeptical eyebrows.

The person she was talking to would pause, testing her with their eyes, admit defeat by revising, and carry on with their story.

With a smile, my wife would thank them for their honesty, letting them know she thought nothing less of them for attempting to adjust the story for her benefit.

All of this with a look.

My wife, who spent so much time focusing on the verbal and the vocal, said all of this with her face.

And after these people had jumped that first hurdle with her, they would talk to her for a long time. My wife made them feel they had earned something and they'd turn that something over to her.

20.

ONE LEG PROPPED UP in the window frame, my wife looked at the view.

We *had* no view from this apartment. A book lay ripped beside the foot that remained on the floor.

She had a cigarette in her mouth. Her hands were a fistful of pages. She was sending them out the window one by one. She crumpled some, sailed some flat and free.

She sent out a puff.

I had just opened the door. I was coming home from work. It was summer, year four and the sky was still light.

This didn't make me nervous, but instead excited. She looked over her shoulder when I came in the door, mumbled a hello from her cigarette-pinched mouth. She turned back to what she'd been doing and threw the cover of whatever book it was down the several stories.

I walked over to her and sat in the chair near the windowsill. "Bad book?"

She smiled, conspiratorially. "*Great* book."

I knew there was some sort of method behind her madness and I knew she wanted me to ask, so I did. "Why tear it to pieces then?"

"My hope is that people will find a page and read it. I hope they'll fall in love with it and look for the book. The author and the title is printed on each page, on either side." She folded a page into a smallish paper airplane, flew it out and away.

I was fascinated, disturbed, intrigued, but not surprised. Wasn't this exactly the type of thing she'd come to make me expect? Hadn't it been little constructed acts such as this that had drawn me to her? When we met, didn't I think the banks of cassette tapes had to be the tip of some insanely creative iceberg?

"What's the book?" I asked. I would read it that night. I would figure out what had made her so mad with passion.

She gathered the pile of paper from the floor in her arms and stepped onto the fire escape. She sent the armful into the air in a flutter. "You have to go down there and find out for yourself. I'm not going to talk about this book, or recommend it. This was my sole act of promotion. This is all I can do."

"Haven't you already messed up this philosophy a bit by telling me how wonderful the book is, by telling me I could go down and get a page, and figure out what book it is? I would be reading it with that expectation then. I'm not just randomly stopping on the sidewalk to pick up a piece of trash."

"So don't go down there, then."

A moment ago I had been fascinated. Now I was seeking loopholes in her grand gesture. Why did I feel the need to ruin this for her?

As usual, I digressed. "I'm not going to go pick up a page. I think it would foil the plan. I'm sad I can't read this book that was so important to you, though."

"So read it! I don't care. This isn't some experiment that can go wrong," my wife replied. "It was something fun I wanted to do."

I had invested more in the act than she had. I had assumed she meant the entire action on some magnificent scale.

She usually functioned at this level.

Just this once, she had apparently wanted to share something in an unobtrusive way, without imposing herself, her opinions on the work.

She had sought to enlighten the world through a random act that could never be tied back to her.

I had made the entire situation reflect her.

And the more I thought about it, the more it seemed she was performing all these acts and tasks of hers at random. She would pick at the beginning of a spool of thread and tire of unwinding it before coming to the end. Only once do I know of her managing to maintain interest until the spool was spinning, naked, but in sight of the huge knot of thread of which it had spent its life being stripped.

21.

MY WIFE FORCED ME TO paint wine glasses one evening. It had been something she'd been talking about for a long time, and one night she had all the supplies laid out.

She said, "We need to do something together. We need to make something. At the same time. We need to start producing."

We had been married just over a year.

She bought the glasses, bought paint and set up a painting party. I was so tired that night, wanted nothing more than to collapse into bed. I didn't want to do something creative. I didn't want to do something silly and sentimental. I didn't want to do anything that required energy at all.

I certainly didn't want to think of some picture or symbol to paint onto a glass that I'd be asked to explain, make meaning where there needn't be any.

What I wanted was *out*.

I wanted *away* that day.

I had come home with the intention of telling my wife I didn't think I could last. I had married her in a blind spot.

My heart was pumping wildly as I turned the key in the lock, anticipating what I had no idea I thought I was going to say.

I was sure it was going to be irreversible. I was certain it was going to hurt her. I knew I would be even more tired at the end of the night.

For weeks I had felt trapped and weighed down.

In the first few months the marriage had been nothing but splendid. I had someone to come home to every day. I had a woman who loved me, who was endlessly interesting, who I dreamt of while she was lying next to me.

As that first year progressed though, I felt simultaneously ostracized and smothered, this being the first occasion in which I ever had to answer to anyone but myself. My wife, I came to learn, was extremely private. She simply refused to talk about certain things and sometimes refused to talk altogether.

And yet there was nothing to accuse her of. Despite these feelings of being left out of some loop, there was nothing concrete that I might point to as evidence. I would leave conversations fulfilled, and then sitting at my desk the next day I would remember a question I had asked her, a simple question that likely could have been answered with a word or a sentence, and I'd also recall how I had never received a response. In the beginning I thought it was possible that I had a terrible memory, but I would tend to ask a similar question again, only to find myself seated at my desk the next day, not remembering the answer.

It was like some conversational sleight of hand. I excused the disappearance of the quarter I thought I was supposed to be following with my eyes in favor of the bunny rabbit she produced from her hat. Only when the bunny was no longer visible did I sit back and wonder where that quarter had gone.

That night I arrived home overwhelmed by this feeling of isolation, of obsession, of a certain sort of deception I couldn't identify. I decided I would tell her how I felt. I would tell her I didn't think I could do what we promised to, that I was wrong and I wouldn't be able to live the rest of my life with her. I loved her, but I was too constantly disoriented.

When I turned the key in that lock, I saw her seated at the dining room table, beaming at me. There was a pizza, plates and eight little pots of paint and a half dozen plain clear wine glasses. There were two cups of water, some mixing trays, fine-tipped brushes. I paused at the door. I must have looked pale. "I thought we could paint ourselves wineglasses." She stared at me expectantly.

I was going to accuse her of not loving me and trusting me, and there she sat with pizza and paint, ready to feed me and make something that could last for all of our life together.

This woman was nowhere near ending our relationship. She believed this was only the beginning. And so, looking at her flip open that pizza box at the table as I shrugged off my jacket and set down my bag, I didn't say a single thing I'd planned to say. My usual cowardly self decided I was too tired that night to try and convince a woman that we didn't belong together, that what she thought was the beginning was actually a well-disguised end.

Instead I smiled back at her and sat down at the table as she put the largest slice of pizza on my plate and then helped herself to the smallest.

I thought I still needed to stand up to something; adrenaline hadn't stopped pumping through my system. I said to her, "I don't feel like painting tonight."

She looked at me as if I were crazy. She challenged me to turn her down again. She said, "Oh, you're painting these wine glasses with me. And we're going to *enjoy* it." She said this with a straight face, and then broke into a fit of giggles. I could tell she was serious though, that she had been looking forward to painting these wine glasses and she wasn't about to let her hopes be dashed.

"I'm exhausted though. I mean, it's a lovely thought. You should paint them yourself. We know I'm a terrible artist," I said, not looking at her, focusing on the last bites of my first crust of pizza.

I saw her hand reach into the pizza box and pull another piece free. She set it on my plate. Not since I was a child had anyone done this. "That's precisely the point," my wife responded. "We can have guests over and let them guess who made which ones and then we can laugh at my pretentious copies of artists, and praise your, at the very least original stick figures and wishy-washes of color. It's the perfect expression of what art is truly valuable. You're not derivative, darling. You're too untalented to even be derivative and that's all that matters to me and to anyone." She chuckled to herself as she bit into a slice.

I was breathing heavily now. I still couldn't look at her. "Perhaps we could do it another time then. I don't want to right now."

Her response was curt and assured. "Nope. It'll take all of a half hour and I will do all the clean-up. I've been looking forward to this all day. We're going to paint wine glasses even if you have a terrible time of it."

We painted wine glasses that evening. Of course we did. I painted messages and tiny illustrations that had no value, had nothing to do with me, in fear that some form of my previous intention might leak out. I painted a glass with a primitive-looking golf ball and putter, with a message that read, "Golf is a good walk spoiled."

My wife cast me a disparaging look. "You hate golf. Tell me you didn't paint that for the irony. I'm so sick of irony."

I didn't respond. She painted a glass with a lacy looking pattern and then, on another, a gradated blend of color that evoked Rothko. I painted a glass with a set of small eyes in large eyeglasses, inscribed, "Free vision tests." On my final glass I painted two outlines of a square. One square met the circumference of the base at four points. The other I painted plainly on the side of the glass.

My wife's last wineglass had on it a rather impressively intricate drawing of a spine, each vertebra indicated with the smallest stroke of her paintbrush. Next to the illustration she wrote the suffix "-less." I eyed her, looking for clues as to its implications, and she smiled proudly.

I begged exhaustion and went to bed soon after, while my wife was still cleaning up the supplies.

It took only a few days before the need for escape passed. It was a hunger that lingered until the point when it could no longer be felt.

22.

My wife and I agreed to housesit for a distant cousin of mine.

It was a mansion on the north shore, but truly old, not one of those awkward new behemoths in a cul-de-sac development.

We were to stay in the house for a week. Their dogs needed daily feeding and we would water their plants and take in the mail.

One could say we were doing it as a favor to friends, but it was a great getaway for the two of us. We were lucky to go on one small vacation a year. The opportunity to housesit fell over my spring break. My wife took off a week from work. We packed suitcases, told our neighbors we would be away for a bit, and drove up to the house. Our eighth anniversary was coming up and we welcomed the escape from our everyday lives.

My cousin and his wife gave us free reign: "Eat what you want. Use whatever isn't behind lock and key. Have people over. Clean up after yourselves when you're done, and it's fine by us."

We were told to stay in the master bedroom. They'd already changed the sheets. It was a massive bed with curtains that shut it off from the rest of the room.

The master bath was, as we should have expected, larger than our entire apartment.

The kitchen was gourmet, and their cookbook selection was elite and extensive.

The living room was breakable-looking yet sturdily restored.

They had a library with a sliding ladder that ran along the bookshelves.

My wife said, "That was my dream. When I was a little girl? I dreamt of gliding along a wall of books."

My wife said, "This is heaven!" She was not being over-dramatic or sarcastic.

The study, a separate room from the library, had a roll-top desk. I had read about roll-top desks when I was a kid and had imagined organizing an entire lifetime within those cubby-holes and drawers.

Once our hosts had given us a tour, had again told us to behave as we pleased, had shared with us the alarm codes and headed off to the airport, we roamed the house on our own.

We found the attic up a narrow, spiral staircase in the back of the house. The ceilings slanted along the interiors of the peaked roof. We tiptoed among steamer trunks and dress forms. We had no idea why our friends would own these items. They were the type of people that might buy this stuff because it was what should be in an old attic. We found a shoebox of old love letters. My wife became entranced. We spent the entire first afternoon and evening in that attic. We found old typewriters and phonographs. An old grandfather clock, in our first hour, startled us with proof that it was still functioning.

My wife wept in the attic that afternoon, in love and over-whelmed.

I played old scratchy big band and jazz records on the phono-graph.

I clicked the typewriter keys.

I found a garden of old music boxes beneath one of the eaves and wound them all to play in a little cacophonous symphony of intricate cylinders.

My wife choked out love letters filtered through her bleary eyes, tripping over words with anxious speed:

> *A Very Valentine for my Gertrude,*
>
> *Thanks for the freedoms that hide beneath our limits. Thanks to mighty age that lets us feel secure in our knowledge. May our parents open their eyes one morning to new knowledge, and tell us to love with all our hearts despite the silly dreams they hold in their heads. May they find new language to say what separates them from us: the first hand from the presumptuous hindsight of practicality.*
>
> *You have placed your finger on my pulse. My heart is beating for the pressure of your touch alone now.*
>
> *Can you imagine a day when our words no longer are a sign of our separation, but more so our reunion? A compensation for all that has been lost in this time when we live under roofs that bear down, rather than lift high?*
>
> *Almost everything is yet to be said,*
>
> *Mason*

My wife looked rapidly between the letter and me, in disbelief, waved the letter around as if it were proof of some argument she was making. "This entire box is like this. There are no letters from Gertrude, but there are boxes of letters from other people, too."

My wife opened another box, began to rifle through them. "But *all* of them are addressed to this house. This is incredible."

I unfolded ancient easels, set old pastoral oil paintings on them, probably once rotated from their spaces on the walls.

I found hope chests of yellowing old table and bed linens and constructed togas and gowns by folding and draping them on old dress-forms.

My wife, new tears streaming down her face, walked over to me, held a new letter tightly in her hands:

Henry! Oh! Henry!

I snorted. My wife shot me a look.

> *In this world, I choose you. I choose red wine stained teeth on an ordinary, unknowing face. Oh! How I laughed the other evening as we drank and your mouth grew a heavy purple lining. (Don't think me unladylike!) I wanted to kiss it from your plump, wet inner lips. I wanted to absorb your color.*
>
> *I am eager to drunken you myself.*
>
> *(Am I being obscene? I am frightened to record these feelings for myself, let alone share them with you. Ignore this! No! I regret none of it!)*
>
> *With the modesty of my signature,*
>
> *J*

My wife and I were both laughing now, with the glee of the innocence of the letter. I wrapped her in my arms. One music box was playing on. The clock chimed midnight. We tucked antiques back into their places and headed downstairs.

My wife was giddy, "What if we left behind an attic like that? What if we became such artifacts? Something for people to find and fall all over themselves with? To hold high in the air and wave around like it was proof of their eternal arguments? What if our desire was chronicled for someone to fall in love with someday?"

"Do we love like that?" I asked. It was a gut reaction. "Does anyone love like that anymore?"

She looked hurt. "Of course! We do especially."

I looked at my wife, changed the subject. "Well, your tapes are that, aren't they? Not the story of our love, but a massive amount of other people's stories that you've taken in, that you've preserved. Don't you think someone will delight in finding all of those someday?"

My wife had noticed how I avoided the topic of our love. She graciously galloped ahead, "Those aren't for the future, though. Those are for the past." She was thoughtful for a moment. She was always denying me my theories. "We'll figure *something* out. Now, I'm going to use up an absurd amount of water to take a bath in that massive tub off the bedroom."

She refused to make the connection, preferred to drop the subject, to go wash the evening from herself.

That night, I read in the immense curtained-off bed, until my wife, returned to me, clean and damp, slipping through the drapes onto the endless plane of the mattress. I went to sleep sure we would spend at least the next day holed up exploring that attic more.

My wife got up before me the next morning. I found only her absence beside me, but laid in bed for a while. She returned babbling about how beautiful it was outside, how we should take advantage of the weather. She dragged me out of bed, into the shower with her. We had our own showerheads in the marble and glass room. We toweled off and lounged around our individual sinks. We were so used to fighting for time under the faucet, for mirror space.

We let the dogs out and chased them around the enormous backyard. We grilled vegetable kabobs for lunch. We struggled to set up a net to play volleyball and badminton and then played for less time than it took to get the net assembled. We remembered how bad we were at both, how not athletic.

My wife and I fell to the lawn exhausted from the fresh air, knees a bit grass stained, noses a bit stuffy from the spring pollen being carried through the breeze.

My wife and I let the dogs lick the sweat from our faces.

We laid there like that through the late afternoon. We watched the sun set, propped up on our elbows, new dew starting to chill through our clothes.

My wife said, "We should share this while we've got it. We should have some friends over here. We should throw a bash! We finally have the space for it! It won't be cramped. It'll be an experiment. What happens when people aren't forced to talk to each other because of proximity? Friday, maybe? What do you say?"

I agreed and said I would call people that night, to make sure they were free.

My wife rolled onto me, excited. She kissed my face, voraciously. "Are we going to be the best party-throwers ever? Are we going to set a new standard for the elite house party?" It was a high-society voice.

I raised an eyebrow. "I think probably not, but is that what we want to be?"

"No!" she exclaimed, grinning, getting to her feet, wobbling a bit, dizzy with plans. "We'll be the most all-inclusive velvet carpet ushers that ever existed. We won't turn a soul away."

"I don't think this is going to be *that* huge, honey," I said, getting nervous. Perhaps we had different ideas of what this soiree would be. We didn't see too many people anymore.

She was already walking back toward the house. "We can dream big!" she shouted, arms thrust in the air, spinning around as she headed toward the deck. She tripped on the second stair.

"Big!" she shouted, righting herself.

I called people that night, asking if they were free. Many were. Some asked if they could bring friends. I told them to tell their friends to bring friends. While I called each name in my phonebook I paced up and down the grand staircase in the entryway of the house. My wife passed by several times, pirouetting across the hall, losing her balance in a twirling chaîné. She pumped her arms in the air, each time I said "See you then" or "I'm glad to hear it." Her enthusiasm convinced me this was going to be good.

We had two days before the party and four days before the owners of the house returned.

We spent the next morning mining the cookbooks for elaborate appetizer recipes. We scanned bar guides for fancy drinks, to offer specialties people wouldn't expect.

We went on an impressive grocery store shopping spree. We didn't want to clear out our hosts' pantries or bar shelves.

My wife and I filled two shopping carts with bottles and jars and loaves and boxes of the good stuff. We had paid no airfare for this trip. My cousin had already insisted on paying us for taking care of the dogs, so these party supplies were to be the only real expense of this vacation.

We spent Thursday preparing food and cooking. We made too much. We knew it. We made mint and cannelloni bean dip to serve with fresh vegetable crudités.

My wife made a buttered nut and lentil dip and breadsticks from scratch.

I prepped smoked fish and potato pate and baked homemade melba toast.

My wife rolled ricotta cheese balls in paprika and chopped nuts and parsley.

We tackled a recipe for Onions à la Grecque.

We baked fennel. We soaked tomatoes in olive oil and garlic and basil. We made crostini alla Fiorentina. We doused mussels in white wine.

We made a mess of that beautiful kitchen, left no utensil untouched, sampled everything, and then cleaned the room from top to bottom.

In the midst of this, the phone would occasionally ring and the friends I had left messages for the previous evening called to say they were or weren't coming. A few were reluctant to give further details of their other plans, when I asked.

My wife and I collapsed on the couches in the family room, leaking the scent of garlic and brine and ginger from our pores. The house was spotless.

The next morning, we felt useless. There was nothing left to prepare.

We pampered ourselves, took a long bath together, sat in the sauna until we were lightheaded and sweaty enough to shower again. We took afternoon naps. We set up the bar. We got out all of the serving plates and spoons and cocktail plates and napkins.

My wife primped in front of the mirror, arranging long strips of fabric around her torso in unpredictable ways. She had on a pair of brown pants that tied around her waist, the legs flapping open on the sides with the help of a draft or a spin. They were wide and thin and flowing. She tied the fabric around her chest again and again in front of the mirror, while I sat on the edge of the bathtub, silent even when she asked for my opinion. I was in awe.

Her hair knotted on the top of her head left everything from the nape of her neck to her lower back completely bare in between arrangements. She was magnificent: a grand line of a woman.

As she spun to express her frustration with how to tie the fabric, the pants billowed out, revealed the length of her legs as well. I swore she was getting longer.

I could answer no question posed to me. I was entirely occupied with the activity of watching her dress. I wanted this to last forever.

She would sigh at my not answering and turn back to the

mirror to rearrange the stripe of fabric around her neck and those pants would spread again in a luminous breeze.

Forgive this flowery speech. The words don't even do justice. There's a not-even-ness to them in comparison with the sight of her.

And what I finally said to her were the words that kept sounding delicately awed in my head: "That back!" And I came up behind her and wrapped my arms around her while she was between attempts at wrapping the fabric.

My wife swatted me away. "How do I tie this?" She was near tears.

"Here," I took the fabric in my hands, and she slouched, limp and upset. I felt the weightlessness of the strip in my hand. I looked at her, evaluating the canvas of her body, and wrapped the fabric around her torso, spinning her to face away from me. I wrapped the fabric leaving as much of her back exposed as I could. I tied it around her neck and kissed her shoulder, again spinning her to see herself in the mirror. She calmed down immediately, a decision having been made.

My wife offered a weak smile as thanks.

"Anytime," I said, and leaned in to kiss her cheek from behind.

My wife turned her head just in time and met my kiss.

We watched ourselves in the mirror, a moving portrait, blinking like shutters flashing, and then the doorbell rang.

The party began later than we thought it would. It began quietly and continued quietly, grew gradually. A few guests arrived right around the time we had suggested, but it was an hour later when the majority showed up. Everyone seemed to think they would arrive in the thick of things. After this next round of people appeared, it wasn't long before the atmosphere grew lively.

And yet the group still seemed smaller than we expected. We

kept pulling each other aside to ask whether some confirmed guest or other had shown up. Many never arrived.

We piped good jazz through the house's sound system.

Spring finches chirped along outside in the garden.

Women's dresses floated like feathers constantly settling around them.

Comments of "You look amazing" and "What lucky weather" spread like wildfire, heating the room to gathering glee.

Men planted their feet, standing in circles, telling jokes, cocktail glasses in hand. They rolled back on their heels as they laughed.

All eyes seemed to linger on my wife and I was convinced it was because she looked so stunning. When we met to check in with each other, it seemed we had an audience. We'd glance out at the eyes, so aware of our every move, and they'd turn back to their conversations.

My wife gave tours of the house, but asked people, politely to remain on the lower level. "We have to return our toy when we're done playing with it, after all," she would remind them, good-naturedly.

Our friends laughed.

A friend said to me, "We haven't heard from you in so long. We're glad we could come. We've missed you."

A fellow professor from my department said, "Your wife is something else. Where did you find such a thing?"

A neighbor said, "You two work well in a large space like this."

Clusters of people gathered around the art on the walls, all up-and-coming names that they weighed the merits of with an embarrassingly thorough knowledge of the art market.

We had strung lights around the backyard fence, and people ventured outside as the night carried on.

People left their shoes in little huddled pairs on the deck and slowdanced on the dew-slick lawn.

Women and men smoked cigars from a box we'd set out on the patio table, ashing into empty cans, perched on the deck railings.

As the air cooled, people returned inside, to lounge on couches. There were separate conversations energizing the living room, the family room, the library. Empty glasses and bottles littered every surface.

People pontificated through their slurred speech on their most honorable life goals, how the magnitude of them had changed through the years, how each year less seemed possible. There were the lucky few who claimed the opposite.

The night went through so many stages.

High school parties when parents were away for the weekend tickled our memories. We felt devious. We felt we might be caught any moment; our parents might come home, furiously sending our friends away, leaving us to our lonely bedrooms, drunk and unfulfilled.

We knew we were safe from this. We knew we were allowed.

Still, my wife grinned at me repeatedly from across rooms like we were getting away with something enormous.

A game of "Truth or Dare" transformed into "Would you rather...?" in the living room.

My wife found she was the only one who would like to spend the rest of her life being older than she was, but she also asked easier questions, ones she didn't care about the answers to.

I watched my wife begin to fidget with the shirt I had tied onto her hours before.

People began to doze during conversations, from comfort and liquor.

Designated drivers gathered coats, jingled car keys.

I kissed, hugged, shook hands with everyone who walked through the door. My wife, visibly drunk and exhausted, retreated to start cleaning up, to scavenge people from the back of the house.

After the last guest waved goodbye as his car pulled away, I shut the front door and sighed with relief.

"My wife!" I filled the house with a voice scratched with the threat of silence. "I believe we might be the best hosts in the entire land!"

I heard no response and pushed myself from where I was leaning on the front door. I headed back towards the kitchen, the family room, "Where are you, my dear?"

The kitchen was still covered in empty plates, in lipstick-rimmed champagne flutes, in cocktail glasses, now full of tinted, melted ice.

"Are you hiding? I want to congratulate you on 'la fete de l'an.'"

She wasn't in the family room either. Perhaps she had truly tired out while I was saying our farewells.

I climbed the front staircase. "My love? My life? Where is my better half?" I called teasingly, still a bit buzzed myself. I peeked into the bedroom: nothing but the rumpled bed where jackets had been piled. I saw the attic door open at the end of the hallway, but the stairway light wasn't on.

"Are you upstairs?"

I walked down the long hallway and found the end of the length of fabric, that had once wrapped her chest, lying on the bottom stair. I flipped the light on. "Hello? Are you up there?" I called and I followed the strip of cloth climbing the winding stairs. I heard a whimper, and climbed faster. A couple of turns around the spiral and I saw her foot, limp. She was on her knees, crawling up the stairs, naked from the waist up, her hair loosened down her back, her shoulders heaving with tears.

I scrambled up beside her, hoisted her onto my lap, "What is it? What happened?" I asked.

My wife wept into my shoulder, dead weight in my arms. I gathered her up, tried to carry her down, but she shrieked, struggling against me. She broke free and continued to attempt to scramble up the stairs, her hands clawing at the treads. When she reached the attic, she caved, fell prostrate on the floor, her torso still pulsing with rhythmic sobs.

I stroked her bare back. I felt helpless. I waited for her to calm down.

I said, "Hush, it's alright."

I traced shapes on her skin. I drew angel wings. I wrote love letters. I rubbed lullaby rhythms against her scapulae.

Eventually she slowed to a sniffle.

"Tell me about it, love. Let's go downstairs and get in bed, and you can tell me everything."

Between gasps: "I don't want to go back downstairs."

"Alright. We'll stay here. Tell me all of it."

"No. I don't ever want to go downstairs. I want to stay *here*."

Sometimes when she was drunk she became irrational like this; my wife would believe in the possibility of fulfilling a desire like this "I want to stay up here forever," she repeated.

"Alright," I said to keep her calm. "Why do you want to stay up here though?"

"I can be old here. We can be old here. I can be as old as I want to be."

"How old is that?" I asked, concerned. I had never seen her this ratcheted up.

She lifted her head, eyes shut tight, but directing her response to me. "Old!" she hissed, and curled in on herself again. "Play me a record. Please! I can't take the silence." I found a jazz album, some old torch singer. She sighed with relief.

"It might be lonely up here," I reminded my wife.

"Good. I can't take anymore youngness," she spat. "I thought this would make all of us feel old and mature, but we regressed to junior high students. It felt like a high school house party. It was disheartening."

"We were all having a good time. You, too. I saw you laughing and smiling. Didn't you have a great time? Everyone loved it." I was trying to figure out where things went wrong.

"I asked if people would like to be younger or older than they are for the rest of their lives and they all said they wanted to be younger." She began to cry again. "They all think the best is behind them. Not one person said they wanted to be older. Not one person said they wanted the wisdom of age. No one said, 'Let me leave this behind.' They all said, 'I wish for *that* time.' They all think they've missed out on something. They'd rather go back and right the past rather than righting the future, than feeling old and new at once. To be newly something else, but to have all of that history behind them. None of them want that. They want to forget. They want to restart. It's tragic. I'm done with them."

"They can't go back though. They're all going to live on. They only choose the other because they know it isn't what they're actually going to get." I was grasping for anything that might comfort her. I unlatched a trunk and pulled out an old lace-edged sheet that smelled of cedar and wrapped it around my wife. "We'll all get to tomorrow and it will be a million times more than we thought it could be. We can't all see it as clearly as you do."

My wife sat up, her face cried clean. She looked at me, exhausted, eyes still a little vacant.

My wife stood, wobbled a bit, and I braced her against myself. She stumbled over to an old couch covered in a sheet to protect it from dust.

The clock struck five. I kissed her forehead. "Did you get any stories from our friends?"

"No," she said, absently. "No, I didn't even think of it."

"Oh, it doesn't matter," I said, silently chastising myself for asking. "You were busy being an excellent hostess. What hostess has time for stories?"

"I don't think I wanted any of those people's stories."

"That's fine, I think." I traced a clump of tear-damp hair behind her ear. "You've told me before, not everyone has a story like that to tell."

I watched her getting upset again. "But one of them must have. At least one of them must have had a story. What was I doing? Passing out appetizers?"

Her eyes welled up and I pulled her to me. "Shhhhh."

"All of their stories were so young. I like old stories. It was like they were trying out new myths on each other. What do they think they'll find?"

My wife said, "They all think they can sustain this youth forever."

My wife said, "They all like the exposition more than even the climax, definitely more than the denouement."

My wife sobbed. "They all want the messy feast so when they look back they'll see the violence of a still life. They want to remember that at least once they were voracious and reckless."

My wife passed out on that couch soon thereafter; I laid on the floor and watched her sleep trying to imagine how I could help her when she woke again. When the clock struck six, she was startled awake. "Let's go downstairs to bed," she said, as if nothing had happened. She let the sheet fall from her shoulders, and I followed her downstairs, hitting the light, still clutching that thin strip of fabric she'd been wearing. I tucked her in and went downstairs to clean the mess before morning woke her.

Sunday our hosts returned to a spotless home. We asked about their trip. They asked about our stay. They told us everything. We told them almost everything, except we never mentioned the attic. My wife and I returned to the city, to our apartment. Monday she and I were both back at work. When I got home that day, she was in her closet.

"Everything alright in there?" I called.

"Mmm-hmmm," came her muffled response. She emerged a moment later, locking the closet behind her, struggling to clasp the bracelet back onto her wrist.

"Let me help," I stepped forward and fastened the bracelet. "How was your day?"

"Wonderful. I feel so rested. I decided I'm going to start painting. I went to the art store and picked up some oil paints and some canvases today and now I have to go to work, but tomorrow morning I intend to start painting."

"That's great." I wandered to the kitchen to make myself some dinner. "Do you know what you want to paint?"

"I think mostly I want to work with objects for a while; I want to start with some elaborate table spreads, you know? Some feasts complete with wild game, big bowls of fruit, some ravished dinner plates. Nothing modern. I want to paint like those seventeenth-century masters."

I was already distracted, comforted by her familiar quirkiness. "What an odd choice. I love it," I said. I rifled through cabinets and then the refrigerator finding nothing at all appetizing to me. "Would you care to paint me a feast right now for dinner?"

"I haven't started yet, but soon," she replied, with a smile.

23.

"CAN I SEE THE CLOSET again?" I asked, at five years.

"You know better," she said, locking it behind her and struggling to reattach the bracelet to her wrist, key dangling.

"Why not?"

"That was a one-time thing. I told you that. You understood. That's the end." She wasn't amused.

"Well, can I see it *now?*" I took on the voice of a pestering child.

She didn't even look at me.

I changed tactics. "No, I'm serious. This is your life's work. You must have filled a few more shelves now. I want to see your progress."

Again, she said nothing.

"Pretty please? I'm not asking to listen to any of the tapes. I just want to see the closet. I want to see the visual growth of the mass of tapes."

This wasn't me being selfish, or it was me being selfish, but it was out of genuine interest in her work.

"The closet is mine," she said, stone-faced. She'd stopped

moving. The closet door was off of the living room. She was standing solidly in the doorway to the kitchen. She was looking for the response of surrender from me that meant she had won.

I wanted in that closet. I felt suddenly entitled. I felt it was something small she could easily do that meant she was letting me in. I stared defiantly back at her.

She was a bit bewildered by my stubbornness. "That closet is mine, and I get *one* thing that is only mine. No, you can't look inside."

This was an unexpectedly harsh way for her to respond to my unprecedented anxiousness about the closet. "What's in there?" I asked, suddenly suspicious. It might have been a clever ruse of her to show me the closet so early on in the marriage so that I might believe the use remained the same.

I stopped myself. I told myself I was being crazy. What did I think was in there? Bodies? Did I suddenly suspect my wife of being a serial killer, smuggling in bones while I was away at work?

My wife never answered the question. I knew the answer. She knew I wanted her to become defensive and open the door.

My wife ripped the bracelet from her hand, breaking the clasp. She whipped it at me on the couch.

I didn't open the closet with that key.

Later when I came into our bedroom to return the bracelet and apologize, I saw that she had bruised her wrist tearing it off. I kissed the tender area as she turned away from me. I strung the key on a piece of ribbon and tied it gently onto her other wrist. She pulled her hand to her, her opposite palm pressing the key flat against her pulse. She never so much as opened her eyes to accept my apology.

24.

MY WIFE CRACKED EGGS.

She usually slept later than I did. My wife worked afternoons to evenings most of the time, and I worked days.

She would wake and watch me get ready, still tangled in the sheets, her smooth morning arms stretching to start feeling the day.

But on mornings after we had gone out together, she woke early, afflicted by some sort of reverse hangover.

I would hear her in the kitchen and get out of bed. I'd sit at the table and watch her take the carton of eggs from the fridge, maybe make some small talk about the night before. But as she squeezed open the Styrofoam carton and took an egg between two long fingers, she would hold an index finger to her lips to quiet me. It was a delicate and distinct process. Two fingers and a thumb on the egg now, she tapped it twice on the side of the frying pan and brought the other hand down to spread the shell and empty it of its yolk.

My wife would set the shell aside on a paper towel and fry up the eggs, scoop them onto a plate, and sit beside me at the table.

My wife didn't eat eggs. She liked the sound of the crack. She liked to make me breakfast, but it was rare for her to cook much otherwise.

My wife making me these eggs seemed one of the acts that I thought proved how true and generous she was, that she would make me eggs when she didn't even like them. I would deny myself the truth of how much I knew she loved the sound of them cracking. I convinced myself it was all for my benefit. I told myself that she made us quiet down before she cracked the eggs to amuse me.

It took me so long to realize very little was done for my benefit.

We would sit as the sun shined brightly through the window, and the way the light hit the left side of her face, I began to see wrinkles, deep furrows forming beside her mouth, the crinkles aside her eyes I admired so lovingly remaining after she smiled. Her forehead was striped with pencil thin creases. Those long fingers I had watched perform their egg-cracking ritual, now fidgeting with a pajama drawstring, were growing bony and form-fitting.

One morning, when I was still avidly testing what I could get away with, two months of married life under my belt, I said, "Tell me a story." And for some reason she granted me my wish.

She raised her eyebrows and those pinstripes thickened above. I never asked my wife for stories. I thought they were something she wanted for herself, but that morning I felt greedy.

"You want *me* to tell you a story?" my wife said.

"Please. I've nothing else to do today."

"I only know true stories," she offered, unsure.

"No true stories. I want a story that's never existed, even in theory." I felt myself getting excited. I was limiting her. "I want a child's bedtime story right now—in the morning."

My wife smiled, energized and nervous. "I don't know if I can."

"One never does." I shook my head, challenging, playful.

My wife held her breath, staring at me.

My wife swallowed.

My wife inhaled and began, as if part of her knew this time would come. She was always prepared. I ate my eggs.

"Once there was a warehouse room that was empty. It had hardwood floors and three steel pillars lining the center of the vast space. The room had four white walls. On the fourth wall, there were four windows. There were many pipes and a radiator, one tiny radiator to heat the entire area. That warehouse wanted nothing more in the world than to be filled with useless objects: with soundless phonographs and tick-less clocks. That room wanted spout-less teapots and halves of saucers, typewriters with irreplaceable ribbons and cracked vases. The room longed to be lined with punched through canvases and oatmeal box cameras. It wanted newspapers too brittle to be opened and read and jars upon jars of keys with no locks. The room wanted objects that were both less and more than they once were. The room was hungry to be filled and silent with clarity. The room stared out its windows at a bleak urban landscape.

"A man began to visit early in the morning. He brought with him a card table and a folding chair. He brought a ladder and a fine-tipped permanent marker. The man brought his jacket and his boots. On his first visit the man began a ritual. The man paced back and forth through the space. He would start at the door and walk along the wall of windows. When he reached the opposite wall he would take one step over and walk in the opposite direction. He would zigzag his way around the entire room in this manner, plowing the floor with his careful, beside themselves, strides. When he reached the opposite corner of the room he took out his marker and removed the cap. He would draw something tiny on the wall, in an area of about four square inches. Each day he would fill another square with something.

Some days it was a gentle little face. Some days a tiny country scene would unfold in the square. Some days he would write a small account of something or other. He would work his way across the wall this way and when he finished a line he moved up and began another. When he could no longer reach he paced his way around the room carrying the ladder.

"On a Sunday he used up his first marker and placed it on the ground in front of where it had run out of ink. He did not finish the picture that day. He left it partially complete on the wall next to a white space and an intricate Spanish-looking design. The next day he began with another marker.

"On another Sunday he finished this wall entirely, and on Monday he began the next wall. The back wall was lined with pens now.

"Each day after the man paced and then drew, he sat at his table and looked at the walls. He set a timer and sat for one hour along the windowed wall, too far away to see any of the individual pictures. He sat, sometimes silent, sometimes humming. During this time the room thanked him for coming each day to help fill it up.

"At night the warehouse was alone. Moonlight shined in, flooding the floor, but never reached the walls.

"The room felt fancy and wild, armored with the drawings the man had covered it with. In a few years the man finished the room. One early morning he brought a camera in as well and took several rolls of film. He tried to get a picture of every section of the four walls, even the portions surrounding the windows. He left once with the table and chair. He returned. He left once with the ladder. He returned. He left once with the camera, his jacket, his boots. Before shutting the door behind him, he set the last, unfinished marker on the ground, outside the span of the door swing. The man shut the door behind him and didn't bother to lock it.

"The room was full. It was painted with pictures and littered with pens. The room was quieter now, with no one to thank, but still content. The room felt still and stagnant. It waited for someone to come and discover the pictures, for someone to appreciate how the room had grown.

"It wasn't too long before a younger man realized the warehouse room was unlocked though, and snuck in. He looked at the walls for hours and brought a girl and a flashlight back with him the next night. The boy's plan worked and the girl fell in love with the boy. Well, really she fell in love with the room, but she loved the boy for showing it to her. The room could tell it was itself that the girl loved, but was happy to help the boy. They came back every night for a week and then the boy invited some other friends to the warehouse. These other friends were too concerned with themselves to recognize the beauty of the room. They made fun of the room and of the boy so that they could feel they were the focus of attention. They couldn't understand why anyone would want to cover a room in tiny pictures like this and leave it unlocked and unprotected. The other kids said that the artist mustn't have cared much. The other kids returned on their own later that night with cartons of rotten eggs, and hurled them at the walls. The crack of the eggs on the walls was deafening. The room smelled awful. The drawings ran in some places, drooping down the walls. In others they turned jaundiced glossy, dribbling yolk, smattered with eggshell bits. The kids left, hooting and hollering, the empty egg cartons confusing the order of the pens on the ground.

"The next day the boy and the girl swung the door open and were overwhelmed by the stench. They took deep breaths outside, and peeked in at the damage. They looked at each other and tears matched tears in each of their eyes. They found clean spots on the walls and kissed the room.

"The boy and the girl walked out hand in hand. They looked back at the building when they were about a block away and kept walking. The room was lonely, but content, because it was still quite full, and all the more beautiful with the addition of the eggshells."

My wife looked down now. It felt like she was finished with the story, but I wasn't sure. "That was heartbreaking. Thank you."

She took my plate with her aging hands. "Good," she whispered.

My wife made me breakfast and told me a story. I was sure she was as generous as wives could be. She exhausted herself.

25.

My wife made a feast of a dinner.

I arrived home late and she was lying on the couch listening to her warped records.

I saw the table elaborately set. Candles had burned to stubs in the candlesticks.

My wife didn't even look up when I opened the door. She stared into the space ahead of her.

I smelled the faint scent of something rich and gourmet. I realized the food must be cold.

The smell was what had soaked into the textiles of the room.

Pillows held the buttery garlic scent of lobster.

Freshly baked bread wafted from the curtains.

The smell of chopped and sautéed vegetables clung to the simple black tee shirt my wife wore as she laid on the couch. Her pants were in a puddle on the ground beside her. My wife's legs leaned on each other, knock-kneed and tired.

The aroma of white wine drifted from the tablecloth, where I saw one of the goblets had been spilled, still laying on its side.

A bowl of fruit sat in the middle, colorful, but whole and unscented.

"Something smells delicious," I said, trying to cover up the fact that I knew I was late.

On the couch my wife continued to stare straight ahead.

"I didn't know you were making such a fancy dinner tonight. What's the occasion?" I said this in a way I hoped sounded appreciative and excited, rather than defensive.

I knew it was not one of our birthdays, our anniversary, or Valentine's Day. This must have been a reasonless act of love and I had come home late, hadn't called.

Now I think, *But how was I to know? She hardly ever made dinner.*

"I'm not mad," my wife said.

To this I had no response. I had made no indication that I assumed she would be. She knew me too well. She could tell that my careful responses were apologetic rather than unknowing. I said nothing.

"Sit down here by me," she said, scooting her legs up further.

I sat down by her feet, ran my hand from her knee to ankle repeatedly. I gave in like I always did. "I should've called. I'm sorry."

"Not a big deal." My wife smiled. "It was a silly idea I had. I thought I might try my hand at cooking a nice, fancy meal for the two of us. I can warm it up. Sit here by me for a while."

"Were you going to paint the table after we ate?"

"I hadn't even thought of that. I guess all that food's still good for something. I could finally make that painting I've been going on and on about. Eh, I'm tired. It's exhausting cooking a feast. Rest here with me and we'll get to work in a minute." Her eyes glazed again.

I was still uncomfortable. "Did you spill that wine glass on purpose?"

My wife looked at me confused, started to sit up and turn around. "Did one of the wine glasses spill?"

"You didn't notice?" I asked. I assumed she'd knocked it over after having been seated at the table waiting for me a minute too long.

Her head turned, her eyes were trained on the spilt wine. I heard her suddenly smell it with a strong sniff. "No. When could that have happened? We need to clean that up before it stains the wood."

"I'll do it," I said, standing, patting her knee. I crossed to the table and began to remove the settings, the plates of food.

My wife turned to watch me. "How could that have happened?" she repeated.

I finished clearing the table and bundled up the tablecloth. I dumped it in the hamper, but the wet spot had whitened the wood in an oddly-shaped splotch already. "Maybe the glass wasn't flat on the table; maybe half of its base was on a piece of silverware or something. It could have tipped anytime. Maybe when I came in." Whenever we shut the door, the whole apartment shook.

My wife's face calmed a bit, but her hand lingered near her stomach, like something had jarred deep within her, like she might be sick.

I went into the kitchen to get a rag and some Pledge.

I heard my wife hum along with the record.

I rubbed at the splotch, but the white darkened only a shade to pale brown, still distinguishable from the rest of the table.

She stood, peculiarly still and meditative. "How odd," my wife said softly. It didn't feel like she was talking to me.

I walked into the kitchen and called to her. "I'm gonna start warming this up in here, alright?" I worked to restore the food to its original grandeur, added a few spices of my own, and my wife eventually joined me, watched me work while she leaned against the sink.

We ate the meal standing at the counter. We never returned to the dining room, never even settled at the kitchen table. We cracked into the lobster on its platter, which was balanced on the burners of the stove. We ate the vegetables from the large bowl I microwaved them in. We pulled off chunks of bread I had warmed in the oven, slathering on butter straight from the wax-paper covered stick, with dull knives. I poured another glass of white wine for each of us and we drank them down quickly; we poured again.

When we had demolished the countertop, the wreckage was severe. It looked as if an army of hungry scavengers had invaded our kitchen.

It was then that we sat down at the table and each pulled a piece of fruit from the bowl.

I took an orange, deftly peeling the skin off in two pieces.

My wife took an apple. She ate it with a knife in hand, slicing off chunks, piece by piece, instead of just biting in. The knife would meet her thumb, and I would watch for blood each time, but she remained unscathed.

We traded with each other, placing slices into the other's mouth.

When we finished our fruit, I asked her, "Sure you don't want to do a modern still life of this mess on the counter?" She looked tempted for a minute, but then I saw artistic ambition give way to the urge to have everything tidy again. She shook her head. We slid lobster carcasses into the trash. We wrapped up the remaining bread. We put the leftover vegetables in Tupperware. We poured out the little wine that was left in the bottle between our two glasses. I washed the dishes; she dried and put them away.

We wandered back into the living room. My wife eyed the spot on the table. "Did you try to get this out?"

I said, "Yes."

"This is the best that can be done?"

I nodded the truth.

26.

I READ A STORY I'd found in an art history book to my wife. We were sprawled on the couch of a bookstore. This activity defined most of our fifth year together: colonizing one or more stuffed pieces of furniture in bookstores or cafes for the better part of a day.

The story I read was an account of why Rodin's great monument to Balzac lacked hands.

"As Rodin was nearing the completion of the cast for what was to be his monument to Balzac, he called a student in to share in his joy and excitement at his progress.

"The student came into his studio and Rodin pulled the sheet from the plaster cast.

"'Master,' the student gasped, 'this statue is truly superb, but, my god, those hands are magnificent! They are surely the most beautiful thing you have ever created.'

"Annoyed, Rodin quickly covered the statue, and ushered the student from his studio, calling a second pupil in to hear another opinion.

"The second apprentice entered and Rodin, again, pulled the sheet from the plaster cast with a flourish.

"'Master,' the student brought his hand to his face in amazement, 'those hands are incredible. They are proof that you are the best sculptor this world has seen.'

"Enraged at the affirmation of the previous student's statement, he grabbed the chisel and hammer from his nearby worktable and in two hard knocks, had freed the hands from the sculpture. They fell to the ground shattering beyond repair.

"'Master, what have you done?' The student fell to the ground grieving for the loss of those beautiful hands.

"'This was not meant to be a statue of hands. I never would have forgiven myself if the world had been distracted from the greatness of Balzac because of the hands I made him.'"

My wife stared at me.

I watched her eyes and, below them, saw something in her lap twitch.

My wife's hands were pulsing in tightly wound fists.

Something was ticking its way up from her lungs.

That something reached her lips and she opened her mouth: "But how was it that Rodin knew Balzac's hands weren't prettier than his prose?"

I didn't respond; I knew I couldn't argue. I knew we would be quiet while we waited for the tension to dissipate. We sat and read silently for a long while. I switched books to try and ease the situation.

My wife cleared her throat. She had something to say.

A bookstore employee cut her off before her first syllable made its way out: "Excuse me, ma'am, but you'll have to put your shoes back on."

My wife looked at this gentleman with an expression that said, "C'mon, really?"

The clerk looked back with an apologetic plea.

My wife untucked one leg from beneath her and slid both of her feet into her shoes again.

"Thank you," the young man said. He continued on to wake up a man in an armchair a few paces away.

My wife turned back to her book and kept reading.

"What were you going to say?" I asked.

She looked at me and searched my face. She was confused. "What?"

"You were going to say something before he asked you to put your shoes on. What was it?"

She thought for a moment. "I'm not too sure." She looked back to her book, then lifted her head again.

My wife said, "Was I going to say something?"

"I'm pretty sure of it."

"Did you *want* me to say something?"

"I *thought* you were going to say something."

"Oh." She looked back down at her book.

I watched her stare at the page for a few moments, and then begin reading again, her lips moving.

I looked back to the magazine I was flipping through, stalled on an article whose title attracted me, called "Wolves at the Door."

Her voice: "I would die on a daily basis if I could. I think that's true."

She could smile so wide. I was *sitting* in her smile, and I admit this reluctantly because there are times when my stomach turns at the thought of that smile, where I regret those smiles of hers so much and wish I could have ignored them and escaped them.

She nodded her head and shifted her position on the couch, kicking her shoes off again and sitting on her feet: "I would die everyday if I could."

I wasn't humoring her this time. "You would be coming back to life though. If you knew you were dying every day, it wouldn't be difficult. You'd know you have more chances."

She wasn't even looking at me, just shaking her head, repeating "Every day," stressing different syllables, saying the words every way she could muster.

I was irrationally angry about the confidence she had in this being some sort of grand statement. "Dying would be nothing more than falling asleep."

Something lit her face anew. "I'd be a man in bed."

My wife said, "I'd be an opera singer. Yvette Guilbert in her black gloves. I'd capitalize on my deficiencies. I'd make a name for myself from nothing."

My wife looked me in the eye, and her face saddened, "I'd fall asleep in the back seat of a car and let someone else drive. I'd stop making decisions, but I'd still get where I needed to be."

My wife grabbed her bag and began rifling through it. She pulled out a pack of cigarettes and a lighter and kissed my cheek. "I'm gonna run outside for a smoke. I'll be right back." She ran off, practically skipping.

It was like she had her own sense of reason. It's such a commonly accepted notion that people have their own sense of humor. Often people with differing senses of humor don't get along very well, but there is the odd occasion where two people with extremely different senses of humor can find themselves in admiration of one another.

I watched my wife through the window of that bookstore and wondered where she came up with the things she did.

I wondered where my wife found the energy to chase after the reasoning she constantly tried out.

I admired it, but I would never understand.

I watched my wife outside that window and her cigarette disappeared quickly. She inhaled and exhaled like a sturdy steam engine, manic with direction and focus.

I watched her drop the tiny stub on the sidewalk, grind it out with the toe of her shoe.

My wife sped through the door and anchored onto the couch beside me.

My wife began: "When I was a kid I had this fear of the opera.

"People spoke of opera as if it were a natural disaster on some grand scale.

"I heard people speak about it like there was no greater punishment on this earth and I heard people make it sound like it was what made life worth living.

"Either way I was sure it was something far too large for me. It was insurmountable. When people even so much as mentioned opera, I equated it with speaking of god. My parents told me never to take the name of the lord in vain, but they never said anything was wrong with talking about opera. Of course, I said 'God' in exasperation constantly and my parents quickly stopped even trying to chastise me for it; they would just give me a look. No one, however, ever noticed that I didn't talk about opera.

"The reason was that I feared what opera could do to me, the way other little children fear the punishment of god if they cry wolf one too many times. I thought opera would find me, and—*change* me, I guess. That was what I was so afraid of. Something was so irreversible about it."

My wife took a sip of her coffee, her hands began to wave: "Everything is bigger: the stories, the voices, the people, the sets, the theaters, the distance between you and the stage. All those people sitting with their flippy little binoculars, squinting towards something enormous. There are so many holes. There's the language barrier. There's the sense that in watching opera one is bridging a gap between the time on the stage and the time this opera was written. And the audience is so far from the action, it's like the delay of starlight. The opera might be over, but you're still glowing with it as the radiance of it travels out to you in your seat. And all of those spans of time are so enormous.

"But I didn't know any of that when I was a child. I had no idea what it even was. It was this thing, *opera*, that people talked about ominously, like it was some omnipotent dictator that could not be brought down. People either loved it or hated it, but it couldn't be touched.

"Now, I'd like nothing more than to be an opera singer. It seems the role to play.

"There are so many things I have been sure of in my life. They have changed so constantly."

She slumped. I stared at her.

"I'm exhausted," I said, and turned back to my book.

27.

AROUND OUR SIXTH ANNIVERSARY, my wife cut off all of her hair. It had been long, to the middle of her back, and a honey blond color she'd never dyed.

My wife donated her hair to have it made into a wig. Her hair had been thick: it was soft and fine, but there were masses of it.

After, she was left with a pixie cut.

My wife had never really styled her hair when it had been long. She washed it regularly, combed it through, and let it fall down her back for the rest of the day. At work, she wound it into a regulation bun to wait on tables.

Now that her hair was short, she filled a once almost-empty shelf of our bathroom cabinet with molding waxes, gels, mousses and sprays. When I came home each day I was always surprised to see how she'd arranged her hair. Some days she matted it to her head. Some days she fluffed and flipped it out. She spiked it, sometimes subtly, other times in a punky mass of confusion. One evening I came home to her lying on the couch, a Mohawk flaring above the pillow upon which she rested her head.

On our sixth anniversary I gave her a variety of barrettes I found in an antique store. I brought an enormous ancient silk flower I'd discovered in a box marked "Miscellanea" and a selection of pillbox hats with netted veils.

Digging through the bins at the back of the store, I'd also secured a variety of scarves she might tie around her head as headbands.

She opened the box before we left for dinner. "We're going to be late now." She smiled.

"Why?" I moved to touch her and she slapped my hand away.

"Fiend! I have to try all of these on and figure out which one to wear tonight."

"Our reservation is in twenty minutes. If we don't leave now we'll wait for a table all night."

She darted into the bathroom with her box of goodies, "So call and ask if they can hold our table or maybe move our reservation down a bit."

I called and they could get us in a half hour later than we'd originally planned. "You have fifteen minutes to primp like a schoolgirl in front of that mirror and then I am leaving whether you're on my arm or not."

My wife appeared wearing a dramatic smile. "Do you like?" She wore the hot pink pillbox hat.

"If I say I adore it, does that mean we can leave?"

"Silly." She straightened my lapel. "You've moved our reservation to a half hour from now. So, do you like this hat? Because if you like it, I have an idea for something else we could do." She pulled me to her by my lapels.

We unbuttoned, unzipped, unclasped. We fell, rolled, fumbled. It felt old and new, exciting and comfortable, deviant and spontaneous. I made many comments about how much, indeed, I enjoyed that pillbox hat.

Although my wife had always called the shots sexually, she called them that evening with the vigor of our earlier years. Lately, she'd become hyper-aware of the posturing involved in lovemaking, how even when genuinely motivated, a moment's objective glance at the situation could pull her out of the action. When she found a way to ignore these thoughts, we were terrific, like we'd been when we began. She found passion and whimsy and belief in us.

We arrived at the restaurant on time, a little mussed, and the maitre-d' ushered us to a table at the back of the restaurant.

We ordered an extravagant meal, beginning with an artichoke soaked in a Brie and mustard sauce. For our entrees my wife had fricassee of chicken and I had marinated steak. For dessert, profiteroles doused in chocolate sauce. We savored each bite, vocal in our enjoyment. About halfway through our meal, when each of us had downed two martinis apiece, a couple was seated next to us. Quite a bit older, probably in their fifties, they glanced over when we both moaned at the first taste of our entrée. We apologized; they laughed. They asked us if our meal marked a special occasion.

"Sixth anniversary." My wife responded with actual joy. Her tongue sprang out to catch a trickle of sauce threatening to spill from the corner of her mouth.

"Is that right?" the woman asked. "This is our *twenty*-sixth anniversary. You both still seem very much in love. So nice to see a young couple making it work so well."

"Thanks," I replied. "Although most of our friends are married, too, have been for a while, and they're all holding strong. I don't believe we're an anomaly."

The woman smiled. "I suppose I hear the divorce statistics and assume nothing works out anymore. This is both of *our* second marriages. We both married while still in college, and neither lasted more than a couple years. By the time we were trying to find jobs and a place to settle, the differences were too wide."

"It's true," the man chimed in. "My first wife and I thought we had it all figured out, and one day she just went crazy, said I didn't care about her goals, only worried about myself. The day I knew it was over she kept shouting, 'When are we going to start thinking about me?' Every decision I made, every word spoken had been for her. I didn't know what to do. We went to a few marriage counseling sessions, and decided we were too young to spend a lifetime making it work. Then I met this one," he nodded at his wife, "and it all came clear. We both wanted to live in the city. She took a job at a gallery. I'm a lawyer. Our life is logical and clean and easy. Twenty-six years of smooth sailing."

His wife leaned in, whispered, "Not always entirely smooth, but certainly better than the first marriages ever could have ended up. My first husband is a high school wrestling coach out in some bumbling farm town. Now tell me, can you imagine me in a farm town?" She looked at us as if we knew her, as if she wanted a straightforward answer, valued our opinions.

I froze, but my wife exclaimed, "Absolutely not. That would be absurd. Look at you. You're a city girl all the way."

"Exactly!" The woman sat back in her chair. "You've known me five minutes and you could tell. How on earth did I marry a man who couldn't see I'd never be a country wife?" She chuckled to herself.

My wife never turned away, wanting to appear polite; she was, I'm sure, loving this odd little encounter.

The woman next to us showed no sign of stopping. The waitress came, took our plates away, our new friends at the next table received their food and the man slowly began to eat. The woman eyed her steak, but carried on as she cut it into ever smaller bites, talking a mile-a-minute. "I'm a reader," she said.

"My first husband followed me around college like a charmed snake. We had nothing in common, but he listened intently to everything I said. I rambled on and on about the work I was doing. I was an art history major. He wrestled. We met in a lit class that we needed to take for a general education requirement. I was a hot ticket back then and he was handsome, friendly, popular. I was arty and exotic, and I had a great body." She held the back of her hand to shield her mouth. "Though you'd never be able to tell now! We were sure we were in love and we'd last a lifetime. He wanted to get married, so we'd never have to hide anything from our families, could begin our lives together. I'd been terrified of commitment and settling down, but for some reason, with this huge decision, I decided to attempt to overcome my fear. After my junior year, we married, a smallish wedding, reception in my parents' backyard. We'd known each other less than a year."

Our dessert arrived. Coffee was poured. While my wife and I spooned mouthfuls of puff pastry, ice cream and chocolate sauce, the woman inhaled the majority of her plate of food. When she'd finished, she continued. "Anyway, we went on our honeymoon: Hawaii. We began living our lives in a little apartment our senior year. He had a collection of sporting equipment he horded in the one communal storage closet. I bought masses of shelving.

"Enter books. Mine. The beginning of the problem. He didn't understand why I had so many. Nor why they needed to cover the walls. He thought the apartment would look so much nicer without all that clutter. He didn't get why I needed to buy the books, why I couldn't take them out from the library. Finances immediately came into play. I worked extra hours to pay for books I wanted to own. He said I was never around and that I never did anything for him. What he meant was I worked instead of cooking him dinner, which I actually did quite often. Not every night, but *often*, and not once did he make dinner for us. He said I should be putting the money I earned toward something for the both of us, or save it for the future. I told him the reason I worked was books. If I didn't buy books, I wouldn't work. I told him, I'm not giving up books for you. We fought about priorities. We were young and foolish. All those times I thought he was interested, even fascinated in what I was talking about, I realized he was just being a good listener, an honorable trait certainly, but I'd been under the illusion that listening implied we would build a relationship marked by fulfilling exchange.

"I kept working. We both graduated. We stayed in the college town for some time after, all the while I tried to convince him that I needed to move back to the city. He nodded, I thought genuinely, but actually, I later learned, dismissively. He thought he had me pinned. He was sure eventually he'd break me, cow me into doing whatever he pleased and he waited me out slumped in an easy chair, expecting me to calm into my domesticated self any minute. One evening near the end, a slow day at the gallery allowed me to go home early. My first husband and I had had a spat the night before, again about how committed each of us were to making the marriage work, our willingness to sacrifice personal pleasures for the sake of our general well-being. Again he'd brought up my books, suggested I sell them to used bookstores, suggested I stop buying more. I came home from the gallery and collapsed in his easy chair. I stared at the book shelves that dominated the living room. They climbed every wall. Almost immediately, I felt dampness sink into the bottom of one pant leg. I felt the seat, cool and wet with something, beneath me. I stood and then crouched beside the chair lowering my face to the dampness.

"It was beer. He'd spilled a beer and made no attempt to clean it up. Upon closer inspection I found a herd of cheese snacks packed into the crease of the seat. Disgusting! I brought a trashcan and some paper towels. I scooped the remaining debris into the waste bin and found a layer of Fritos, a layer of corn chips. Under that, deep in the groove, I brushed out anonymous grime and lint. I scrubbed the beer stain out. Then I disposed of my tools and I looked again, standing this time, at all of my books. I was feeling dramatic. I began taking the books down in stacks. I brought them to our bedroom first and laid them end to end, overlapping so no space lay between them. I opened each to a random page, covering the floor, the bed, every horizontal surface. I did this in every room of that tiny apartment.

"By the time I finished, my books blanketed the place. Every surface covered. Every binding broken. The content of all of those books released into the air. All the theories, images, stories I'd processed in my lifetime, lay around me and sang out their silence together, pages shuffling. I sat on the couch, and looked over them, this miraculous garden of my notes, my influences, and I heard my husband fumbling to turn his key in the lock. I heard him twisting and pushing the door in at the same time.

"I had laid the books all the way to the door. He had to add a little pressure to swing the door open against the books' resistance. When he came in, I grinned, Sheherazade laying out all one thousand and one stories in one night, asking for it. I smiled with the relief of an ending. Surely, this had to be the last straw. 'What the fuck is this?' he asked.

"I said nothing. I had no answers to give, no approximations I thought even remotely appropriate. I sat and grinned, let words I'd read speak, pipe up into the air from their grounded pages."

The waitress came and took their plates, asked if they'd like a dessert menu. The husband nodded. My wife and I had our coffee cups refilled. We were no longer humoring this woman; we were riveted.

"He kicked some of the books, furious at the state of the apartment and my silence. 'What the fuck does this mean?'

"I sat and smiled, tears dripping down my face. I knew they'd be fine. Even if pages ripped, they could be taped. The wear they withstood in this beating would only add to their history. Several books of theory he shredded —the fiercest deconstructionist critic I'd encountered, that hillbilly man I'd married.

"I cried through my smile, and when he finally tired and swept the books off his easy chair, he said, 'I don't know who you are. What on earth is this all about?'

"We cleared books off our bed and slept, tired and settled. Early the next morning we woke and without turning to me, he said, 'I thought we wanted the same things.'

"'Didn't we both, though?' I said. I'd been sure of it myself. 'At least we could figure out how wrong we were together?' I offered.

"'Some consolation prize,' he said. 'My wife chose books over me. How do I explain that to people?' He turned then as if he wanted a real answer.

"'You don't,' I said. 'People don't need the world explained to them. You need the faith that they're smart enough to see with their own eyes, and that the only truth is the one they construct on their own.'"

My wife and I sat. Our neighboring table's dessert arrived. The woman looked rather abruptly down at her slice of pie and didn't turn back to us. She picked up her fork.

My wife and I had no idea what to say. The woman ate her pie. Her husband downed his slice of cake. As if they had come to some bizarre agreement, neither looked at us. We continued to look at them, but they never made eye contact again.

Neither of us knew how to proceed. Leaving might be rude. Our coffee cups were filled for a third and fourth time.

The couple didn't speak. When both had finished their desserts, the waitress brought their check. They paid, politely responding to her. They looked at each other for affirmation as they straightened themselves. When they stood to leave, shuffling between our tables, my wife took the initiative. "Nice to meet you," she said. "Have a lovely anniversary."

Neither of them turned or acknowledged my wife's well wishes in any way. It was as if she had said nothing.

My wife stared at me.

"What was that?" I asked.

"I'm not sure. Maybe she needed to get that out?" My wife's face wore confusion, anxiousness, maybe a bit of humor.

We walked into the unusually cool summer night mostly silent, unsure how to process what had occurred. Instead of taking the el the two stops to our house, we walked home.

At our apartment building, my wife fumbled for her keys and I knelt to pull a piece of soiled and torn paper from beneath the bushes lining the walkway.

As my wife pushed into the entryway she looked back to eye me and the page.

We brushed our teeth, washed our faces, climbed into bed. With the lights off, my wife's breathing quickly regularized itself into sleeping sighs. I slipped out of bed and crept to the night table on her side, where I'd placed the piece of paper I'd found.

It was a page of a book, a few lines underlined, and some marginalia. Evidenced by the handwriting, my wife had been the annotator. I shuffled back to my side of the bed, and after listening to her breathe for a long time, fell asleep.

28.

On weekend days during the summer, of our fourth year in particular, we would pack a cooler, pack a bag of towels and books, and head to the beach. Often we'd ride our bikes there, but there were days when we decided to walk the two miles to the lake.

As we got closer the sidewalks got more and more crowded. If we were on our bikes we stayed in the street. If we were walking we parted now and then for the children darting between us. Rollerbladers sailed past, my wife marveling every time at their balance. She, in her clumsiness, had never gotten more than a few squares of cement before tumbling from her height to her knees, jamming the heels of her hands into the ground, imbedding pebbles in her joints and standing again to brush them away. "They move so fast!" my wife would say and look to me for some answer she knew I didn't have. I wasn't much better.

When we arrived at the long strip of walkway that ran along the miles of beach, we'd have to wait for a break in traffic. We'd wait for the bikes to whiz past, for the rollerbladers to glide by, for the runners and joggers to get ahead, so we didn't break their pace.

We never got up early on these summer mornings so the beach was crowded by the time we got there. Broken by docks at which boats never arrived, the first few spans of beach were always packed with people, blanket to blanket, masses of little children weaving in and out between them.

We were in no hurry, though, and so we walked down lengths of beach before we found one that was not so crowded, that seemed a little bit quieter, one where we might relax. Again we crossed through the oncoming traffic to the warm sand, where we kicked off our shoes, and gasped at the heat beneath us. We limped quickly toward the water. We threw our bags down and spread our blanket wide. We whipped our clothes off hastily and raced to the water.

Both of us had been the children who never had the patience to put on sunscreen when they first arrived at the pool. The temptation was too great, and, as kids, we would feign the contentment of setting our beach towels down at the perfect spot, and then throw ourselves into the water with abandon, often shocking ourselves with how cold the water was compared to our warm expectations. We were relieved that both of us had been that child in the group and that neither of us had ever outgrown those instincts.

We agreed that the best part of going to the pool or the beach was the first moment of getting into the water, before you had time to realize how cold it was or to become bored with the floating and splashing.

We raced to the shoreline, didn't stop when our feet hit wet sand or when we were ankle deep in the freezing water. We didn't even stop when it was deep enough to begin swimming. We swam until neither of us could touch the bottom. We dove beneath the water and played shark, circling each other beneath the surface. We swam back a ways to where we could stand again, teeth jittering, refreshed. My wife's long arms now visible above the waterline were covered in goose bumps, and I'd hug her to me for a long while, both of us shivering. I'd keep my arm around her waist as we battled the small waves back to shore.

We would lie on our blankets, still chilled from the cold water living in our skin, but it was never long before the sun baked us dry, and the glisten of sweat would twinkle again along our hairlines; a trickle would escape the crease behind our knees. We'd roll over and let the light shine on our backs, propping ourselves up on our elbows to read books that had waited on the shelf all year.

I watched as stray hairs fell forward, dusting watermarks onto the pages of my wife's fine hardcover books. I would wince at the stain, lean across and brush the hair back behind her ear. She'd look at me and smile, thinking I was being tender.

I'd lie down and let my eyes rest, heavy from the fresh water drying on them and the overwhelmingly bright sun. Inevitably I would doze off, the sound of plastic shovels in sand and the hiss of pop cans cracking open on all sides.

When I awoke, she was always gone. I wouldn't worry. I knew she couldn't be far. I knew she liked to swim and that she didn't like it when I swam with her or watched her. I knew my wife liked to swim for herself.

When I tried to swim with her, she'd say, "This is not a competition. I know I can swim faster than you, but I don't want that added stress. I want to swim against myself."

When I'd watch her swimming, whether I was in the water with her or lying on the shore, she'd later tell me, "I don't need an audience. It screws up my stroke when I know someone is watching me. Let me feel lonely and private when I swim. For once let me forget that there is always at least one set of eyes on me from some direction or another."

So she started heading out for her swim when she knew I had fallen asleep on the warm sand. More than once, when I was resting my eyes, she'd whisper my name to see if I was out yet.

"Go swim. I'm not moving for at least twenty minutes," I'd grumble, half-asleep.

She wouldn't move from her spot, though. She stayed put until I was truly asleep.

When I awoke, I would sit up on the blanket, and watch for her to return. I knew I wasn't supposed to do this, but I didn't care.

Of course, I would see other swimmers before her and think they were her, only to have them approach and show themselves to be other than my wife.

When she was close enough I could tell by the color of her hair, whipping about as she came up for air. I could tell it was my wife because of the glimpses of her swimsuit that snuck above the water when she took an unevenly large stroke.

My wife found her grace when she swam. There is no falling when one is in water. My wife did not have to go up or down in the waves, she hovered near the surface and moved with assurance. Gone was the fear of a misplaced step that so often brought her down to the ground.

When my wife emerged from the lake, slow and dripping, she would set her eyes on me, warning me, threatening me because she knew I'd been watching her. "Flawless," I'd say. "And I've been watching for sometime."

She would push my shoulder playfully. "You know better," she'd say and lower herself down onto the blanket, ribs rising and falling with an exaggeration only the weight of water can cause.

She changed the subject. "Once, there was a woman with maps covering her skin. They weren't tattooed onto her or anything. They had just been there as long as she could remember. Looking at pictures of herself as a child, there were no maps on her skin, but looking at photos of herself when she was a bit older, out of school, she saw them in every photo. They hadn't formed lightly and darkened with time. They had suddenly appeared, though I remind you that the instance in which they showed up for the first time was not significant in any way, and she did not remember it.

"Sometimes, in boring situations, like watching insufferable romantic comedies or listening to her boss explain the importance of not using the office copy machine for personal business, she would stare down at the exposed parts of the map, on her arms and legs. She would stare longingly at locations, wondering where she was supposed to go, knowing if only she were ever told, she would have the means of finding her way there.

"Other people never brought up the fact that she had a map on her skin, though on occasion she caught people staring curiously and then looking away in public. The map was in no way natural looking. It did not look ancient in a way that might have been misconstrued as some sort of birthmark. It looked like a modern road map. She was unaware of where in the world the streets and roads lining her body might be located, and she never researched where the names might have a common bond, because she never knew exactly what good it would do.

"For the most part the woman liked the map, saw it as something that differentiated her from the rest of the population, and memorized directions from the street above her left breast to the one that ran parallel to it below her right ankle. She memorized other routes as well, but this was her favorite because these two locations – dead end side streets, running one way – seemed the most difficult to find a way between.

"In bed, her husband traced paths along the map, lightly running his index finger, his tongue from her ear to her navel, never cutting between streets, turning at right angles, sometimes rounding corners that caused him to arrive in the least efficient way possible. The woman narrated the directions he was taking. A compass graced the skin of her right hip, indicating which way was north.

"The woman did not know the maps on her back as well as the ones on her front. In the mirror, she attempted to memorize the names, but her neck would tire from craning around, and her eyes would strain from trying to read the names backward. Her mind twisted as she tried to convert east and west through the confused left and right of her mirror image. She would give up sooner rather than later, her hair not yet dry from the shower she had just taken.

"One day the woman was lost and unsure of how to find her way home. She stopped at a gas station, but the attendant didn't know how to help her. He had never heard of the town she said she'd come from. 'Where am I now?' she asked and the man named first the town she was in and then the intersection at which she was located. She recognized the street names from the back of her neck, but did not remember where they were in relation to any of the streets on her front. She asked the attendant if she might use the bathroom and he handed her the key.

"She looked in the mirror and saw nothing but herself. Her clear skin was unblemished by the map which had covered her for so long. She began to weep. She turned around to look at the back of her in the mirror, hoping to see the streets the man had named on the back of her neck, but there was nothing there either. She emerged from the bathroom and asked the attendant if he had seen maps on her skin when she had entered the gas station. The man squinted his eyes at her and said, 'Maps?' She asked if he had a map of the surrounding areas that she might use to determine how to get back home. She knew she had not gone far. Wherever she was, she had walked there.

"The man brought out an atlas, but she could not find her town anywhere on the map. She searched for towns that she knew were near her own, but found none of those either. The man asked repeatedly if she was alright. She wept onto his atlas, large watermarks marring the broad pages, and he pulled the atlas away, stashing it again under the counter.

"The man asked if he could call someone to come pick her up. She recited the number of her home telephone, but an automated operator informed first the attendant and then the woman that the number had been disconnected.

"The woman was at a loss. The attendant sat her down behind the counter while she cried. An older woman, who had filled up her car outside came in to pay for her gas, and asked what was wrong. The attendant informed the older patron that the woman was lost. The woman heard the attendant whisper what she had said about there once being maps on her skin. The older lady craned her neck around his shoulder to get a look at the lost woman, still crying but quieting down to hear what the man was saying about her. 'Isn't that always the way?' the old woman called to her.

"The woman looked quizzically back at the old customer. 'But who needs a map of where you've been or where you are? You should be looking for a map of where you're going.' The old lady winked and walked out. The lost woman slumped, breathless and unsure behind the counter, as the attendant turned to tell her she couldn't stay there much longer unless she bought something." My wife turned her head toward me.

"Where did that come from?" I asked, surprised, a bit lost myself.

"Came to me while I was swimming. I feel like I've heard it somewhere before, but I can't remember where." My wife brought a hand up and looked at it. She held her hand in front of her face, palm facing out, still pruned from her long swim. I held my hand up to hers. Our palms touched. "We might be told where we're going before we even know the place exists," she said, avoiding my eyes.

"It's true," I replied, "but if we never know what that place is, why bother thinking about it? Who needs a map when you're already being carried there?"

Her fingers closed around mine. Our hands fell to the sand between us, grains clinging to her damp wrists.

"I guess that would be the case if you never wanted to return." Her hand pulled away.

29.

CARYATIDS FASCINATED MY WIFE.

She wandered museums admiring the weight on their shoulders, her favorite those that appeared close to being driven into the ground by their burdens.

In a sculpture court of salvaged caryatids, she composed extemporaneous bad poetry. "Oh caryatid! Crumpled from your contrapposto! Hair flung free and body cramping from resolution!"

She affected faints and melodrama for these ancient women and I laughed, knowing it's what she wanted.

She latched onto my arm and we walked, her hand tightening when we passed one she particularly liked. It had recently rained. The pavement was still damp in spots.

We sat on a cold bench and my wife smiled at an old man leaning on a cane.

"Look at that smile," he said. He turned to me. "You see that smile every day?"

I grinned as well. "Every day for the last two and a half years I most certainly have, sir."

"Sir?" He huffed. "Is my father around here somewhere? I've never been a sir, and I'm not going to start now." The man looked to be at least eighty years old.

"My apologies. Just trying to be respectful."

"Age shouldn't immediately demand respect. Let that be your lesson for the day, boy." He frowned merrily, looking past us to a caryatid, then turned again. "May I sit down?" My wife raised her eyebrows at his forwardness, then scooted enough for him to take a seat next to her. "These statues are lovely, aren't they? An entire garden of caryatids, can you imagine? Did you know that? That they're all caryatids?"

My wife nodded, "That's why we came. I love them, the idea of a form made to bear all that weight."

The man was out of breath from walking. His chest rose and fell laboriously; he coughed when he tried to slow himself. "Magnificent, aren't they? People obsess over the strength of men, they retell the story of Atlas holding up the world, Sisyphus pushing that rock up the mountain, but look at these women. Show me the man who could so elegantly hold up his half of a lintel. Look at the pyraxilean s-curve of that torso, how one hip juts out, how she tucks one shoulder. The substance of her, how could anything be more beautiful? You know, my wife was like that. Never asked me to open a jar for her, always got a stepping stool if she couldn't reach something. When we were first married she carried a child on each hip for months at a time."

"They're very *real* figures, aren't they?" My wife said. "Women strong enough to hold up buildings need mass, some curve for balance." She looked at me, then back at the gentleman. "Which is your favorite?"

The man thought. "Definitely the one crouching in the corner. It's the most honest. It says what the rest avoid. Eventually a woman collapses under the weight. You probably

MY ONLY WIFE | 125

think I'm pessimistic, but it's the end of this kind of story." He rose and walked toward the far corner of the courtyard. When he was a few steps ahead, my wife stood to follow him. I sat on the bench a moment before I got up, too.

Once caught up to the old man, my wife said, "This one, huh?" She made a slow circle around the statue.

"Absolutely," the man said. "See the twist of her neck? Her arms have given out, and now the stone grinds against the delicate bone of her clavicle. Every second she wonders if she should let the weight drop, but she suffers on. Out of pride, perhaps, or duty at any cost. What's tragic is her only escape now is to collapse, and it's sure to crush her. She hasn't the strength simply to set it aside. She's waited too long. She'll become a victim of her pride."

My wife examined the statue as if evaluating weak spots on the woman's frame, wondering what would give next. "So you think she should give up?" she asked.

"Well, for the sake of her survival? Yes. Who cares about pride when you're dead?"

My wife walked to my side, took my arm. She was still smiling. "Not pride," she said. "Honor." As we walked away, she called back: "Pleasure meeting you. Stay warm out here."

She guided us through the double glass doors and the old man called out, "I see it now. It's a tricky smile, fella. Watch out."

My wife pulled the door shut behind us. "He's right," she said. "Age shouldn't immediately demand respect."

30.

My wife relayed to me a story told to her by an elderly woman in a grocery store. My wife had slipped on some smashed grapes near the woman's cart, and though the woman was too feeble to help her to her feet, she told my wife a story, while my wife inspected her skin for bruises and her clothing for wet spots.

The woman told my wife a story about an eyeball that wanted to be a person very badly.

My wife, for once, was in a bit of a hurry. Though she was tempted by this interesting old woman, she tried to walk away when she saw that she was unharmed and clean, but the old woman held her forearm with one hand while bracing herself against her shopping cart with the other.

My wife will now admit that she was slightly frightened. The old woman began to tell my wife how the eyeball would roll around the schoolhouse, trying to tell people that it was indeed human and not just an eyeball, but it had no voice because eyeballs have no mouths.

Again, my wife said, "Excuse me, I really must go. I'm in a rush. Thank you for your concern, though."

The little old woman held on and continued. She told my wife about how someone picked up the eyeball and put it on a desk at some point, so as not to kick it around any longer. This had been the only way the eyeball had traveled on flat surfaces, as eyeballs have no legs or arms, or muscles of any sort to propel them through space.

The desks were slanted slightly though and so the eyeball rolled down the desk onto a desk chair. The eyeball was elated. Now it felt like a real student.

As class began, the teacher asked a question to begin discussion and no one knew the answer and so no one would make eye contact with the teacher.

The eyeball, however, could do nothing *but* make eye contact. The teacher, not recognizing this new student, pointed to the eyeball, and said, "You there. Do you know the answer?"

The eyeball simply stared back, astonished and small.

The eyeball had done the reading. Faced with a page, what else could an eyeball do? But in response to the teacher's question, there is only so much that can be said with a look. The teacher assumed the eyeball didn't have the answer because of its silence.

"Do your reading next time," the teacher said. "All of you, do your reading next time." Pointing at the eyeball, she continued, "Let that embarrassing case of ignorance be a lesson to you."

The old woman had completed her story, but still held on to my wife.

"What does that mean?" my wife asked, not so eager to go now.

"You know better than to ask such a question," the old woman said, wisely. "I say, grapes, eyeballs, what's the difference? They're all slippery suckers and I'm still older than I've ever been."

"Are you here alone?" my wife asked.

"You don't have to worry about me, young lady. That logic of mine has carried me home many a time." She winked and let go of my wife. She hobbled toward the vegetables, and my wife headed toward the meat section. My wife slipped again, this time on some coolant in a refrigerated aisle.

"I'm still older than I've ever been," my wife repeated under her breath, before she gathered herself up again, this time slightly bruised.

31.

My wife walked more quickly than I did.

It was raining out and I liked the rain. I lingered behind her, dancing like a talentless Gene Kelley.

My wife enjoyed walking in the rain as well, but she altered her pace for nothing, for no one. She walked ahead, and I traced her path, not keeping my eyes on her back a few paces ahead, but on the momentary footsteps she left in puddles. I swear for an instant I could see a footstep on the pavement—the shape of her foot in the rainwater lining the gutters.

I was entranced. It didn't happen every time. I followed them closely and I picked up my pace so I maintained the same distance behind her.

"Hurry up," my wife said, unaware I was so near. "I'm freezing. All I want is my warm bed."

"This is amazing," I said. "You're making footprints in water!" She had no idea what I was talking about. She glanced back but she didn't stop. She continued to walk forward, maybe even speeding up. The quicker her strides left the ground, the the *easier* I could see this phenomenon loiter behind her.

When we began to walk under a section of sidewalk dominated by awnings I caught up to her. I pulled her arm around and she almost lost her balance in the sudden stop.

I pulled her to me wrapping my arms around her waist. I traced the path of a cold raindrop down her cheek with my warm fingertip. "You were making footsteps in the rain," I lifted her chin a bit. "I think that might be impossible." I kissed her lips softly. Her arms wrapped around my neck. We had been married two years and I still felt surprised and lucky that I had found a way to make her mine.

When the kiss pulled apart a little, her lips still brushing mine, she exhaled into me, "I think that you might be crazy." We kissed again and again, rain running from our hairlines, cooling our mouths. We wrapped each other like pythons. We warmed under that awning.

The white noise of our focus on each other alone drowned out the sound of the rain.

After the intense, lengthy kisses had faded to little brushes of lips, tickles of cheek to cheek, I whispered, "I think the rain might be stopping." I hugged her close to me for a while longer.

We let ourselves drench each other for a moment and when I took her hand in mine, when I pulled her past the drip of the awning's edge, I took a few large steps ahead. "Watch me walk. See if I can do it, too. Do I make footprints?"

I tried to walk, with my head turned to see my wife's reaction. She said, "No, no footsteps." She apologized with her eyes.

I slowed a bit, though I knew her pace was quicker than mine and she would have caught up with me had I carried on. "Are you sure?"

"The sidewalk is maybe a bit drier now."

"No," I relented and smiled. I let her fill in the meaning. She took my hand and jumped, tall into the next puddle. She splashed us both, soaked the little that had remained dry.

32.

My wife took a class in still life painting. She had been painting for a while, but thought her work was missing something. She signed up for a class, hoping to learn the rules so she could forget them. She wanted the pressure of guidelines and a teacher so she could work against them.

She was obsessed with the idea of the still life. She liked thinking about the aggression of the painter. The trick with a still life is that it cannot be still at all. There must be something in the painting that has movement and rarity to it.

Ultimately what my wife had discovered was that the life of a still life had to come from shadows, reflections, an object that looks like it has so recently been thrown down upon the table that it might still tremble with reverberation. Overturned wineglasses in still life paintings have to appear as if the wine flowing from them is still swelling an ever wider stain beneath it.

This brutality is why entire game animals so often adorn the tables of still lifes. There is a certain energy to the recently dead. There is a liminality to an animal which has been killed but not yet eaten. The space and time in which it resides is potential and riveting.

My wife took this class and came home claiming she might not return for the next session.

I told her if she had paid the class fee already she should at least give it a second chance.

I asked her, "Why?"

My wife said she had already taught herself all of the lessons the teacher had to share.

I reminded her that this had only been the first class and he was bound to venture into new territory eventually. I suggested she tell the teacher her past experience and perhaps he could give her some further guidance. He could suggest some new approaches with which she might attack the genre.

I was the one who convinced her to stay in that class.

She smiled at me, the ever-logical presence in her passionate world. She nodded her head in agreement and flipped around the painting she was holding in her hands. It was the still life she had been working on that night. A skull, an open sepia-paged book, a golden goblet, a hunk of cheese: these were the objects of still life.

"No choice in what you were allowed to paint, huh?"

She shook her head.

"That's a great book, no matter what. I think that was worth the whole class-time. It's beautiful."

She smiled and flipped the painting back around to herself, examining the book. She nodded, she leaned toward me and kissed me.

I loved her.

She tried the class again, and the next week came home empty-handed.

"Where's the new painting?" I asked.

Her eyes turned to mine, tired but excited. It looked like this week's class had taken a lot out of her, "It's not done yet. I did what you said. I asked him for some suggestions about approaching the still lifes in other ways and this time he told me I could imagine a context for the objects we were painting. I could reposition them in my painting any way I pleased as long as it looked correct as far as proportions, shading and perspective go. I'm much happier. It's a much more exciting class now."

I pulled her to me, stumbling her backwards to our couch. "I'm glad to hear it. What kind of art teacher would he be if he didn't let you do whatever you pleased?"

She rested her head on my shoulder, she wrapped her arms around my chest. "Probably a good one," she said, with a sighing giggle.

The next week she was again empty-handed, and by the week after that I no longer expected her to come home with the painting, but I did still ask her about it. I was intrigued and anxious now. It was going to be astounding. "So... where is it?" I asked.

"It's almost done," she said.

"How's it going?"

I needed some more information, but she offered up nothing: "It's going well. I'm anxious to have it finished, though. I'm getting a little creeped out spending so much time with it. I feel I'm in the painting working my way out. The instructor says that's natural. He says that obsession often precedes completion."

"So what's it like inside the painting?"

She was elusive. I kept my eyes trained on her, worried she might disappear. "Come on, I can't *describe* it. My instructor did say the most interesting thing to me today though. He asked me if I was an auditory person. I told him I definitely was and asked him why he wanted to know. He told me the painting called up in him a keen sense of synaesthesia. When he looked at my painting he heard something. He said he didn't want to sound like some crunchy-granola art teacher but there were dull sounds that entered his head when he looked at my painting. I asked him what they sounded like and he said perhaps a saw being played as an instrument, you know, that whining coo. He said he heard a babble of low voices, but he couldn't distinguish what they were saying. He heard the consistent chime of a grandfather clock. Isn't that wild? I hear nothing when I look at my painting."

"That is bizarre. I can't wait to see it." It was all I could muster to say at that point.

She looked at me, like I had suggested something she had never considered possible. A small smile turned up her lips ever so slightly and she gave a half-nod, unconvincing.

The next week was the final class and I expected her to come home with her work so that I might hear all the echoes it had to offer me. She walked in the door, once again empty-handed, and winked. She walked to the record player and put on a record before she laid down on the couch.

"Where's the painting?" I asked.

"My instructor wanted to keep it, so I let him. He told me synaesthesia is a rare, rare thing and if someone ever claims to experience it in your work, you should make sure it's that person that comes to own it." She relaxed a bit after saying this, closed her eyes.

"Wouldn't that be distracting, to have a painting that babbled at you every time you looked at it?" I could see her eyes roll under their lids. "*I* wanted to see it though. I wanted to *hear* it. Couldn't you at least have brought it home for a little while? Can I go see it?"

She opened her eyes. "Look, I didn't know it mattered so much to you. I don't really want to hound this man down now. I already gave it to him. It's his to do with as he pleases."

I was exasperated with her and with all the work she created. "But you worked so hard on it."

She closed her eyes again, "That's right and now I can do whatever I want with it. I gave it away. I didn't want it in my life. It was too powerful. It made me uncomfortable. I'm tired. I'll tell you about the painting some other time, alright?"

This didn't seem like it should be a big deal. I had the sense that I was behaving like a child, but I didn't want to give in.

She looked so peaceful there on the couch, so I sat and I watched her rest. I thought she was spent for the night. In a few minutes though she sat up and reached into the drawer of the end table. She pulled out her tape recorder and went into our bedroom.

She was going to give a tape more of the story than I would ever know.

33.

MY WIFE SLAMMED THE CLOSET door shut.

She locked it up tight.

She fell back against the door, scrambling to fasten the bracelet back onto her wrist.

"What is it?" I asked, startled at the fuss.

"I shouldn't have gone in there today. It's too much."

"Are you alright? Did something happen?"

She gathered herself quickly and forced a smile, nostrils flaring. "No, I'm fine. I need to go to work. I'm late."

I called after her as she went into the bedroom to change into her white tee shirt, "But it's Saturday." I was whining. I wanted an evening with her.

"I always work Saturday. Saturday is date night. That's when the world needs waitresses most." She searched for her keys in vain on the coffee table, the end table.

"Kitchen counter," I said. She stalked into the kitchen, her feigned composure breaking in her frantic effort to leave the apartment.

"Thank you," she said, smiling again as she emerged from the kitchen, forcing a calm appearance. "I'll see you later tonight.

If you go out, leave a note." She wandered over to the couch, now seeming like she had all the time in the world, had nowhere to be. She kissed me, sweetly and softly. She said, "Bye, love."

She casually swung open the door, stepped out, and slammed it violently behind her.

34.

My wife and I went to a bar. In a year she would disappear completely, but I had no way of knowing. By then I believed inertia might carry us on through to the end of our lives.

That night we ordered drinks.

To the bartender my wife said: "Vodka...vodka."

To the man beside her my wife said: "A smoke if you've got it."

Lipstick smudged onto a filter. A match sparked. Two people turned away from each other. I met my wife's eyes as she exhaled.

That night my wife took on a trinity of conversation tactics:

My wife answered questions with questions.

My wife connected topics in a take-a-penny-leave-a-penny manner, dropping off irrelevant remnants of discussions she knew I would pick up and resurrect along the way.

My wife delayed her side of the conversation with attempts to tie maraschino cherry stems into knots with her tongue.

At first she was adept, remarkably talented at this latter feat, pausing only moments to tangle the stem.

As her tongue grew thick with liquor, the pauses stretched, until she spat out a stem, untied, and admitted defeat. She folded her arms, resting them on the bar, and turned to me. She amused herself.

Then I asked the question. "What's in your closet?"

She rested her forehead on her arms for a moment.

As the bartender passed, she lifted her head. To him my wife said: "Vodka, please." The bartender looked at me and I shrugged. To me, my wife said: "That is the *least* of our problems."

I asked again, "What's in your closet?"

She mocked me, "What's in *your* closet?"

"What closet?" I responded.

Sip. "Everyone has a closet. What have you got stacked in yours? You know what's in mine. I never bother you about yours. I don't even ask what's inside, let alone ask to see it."

I was drunk, too, but not as drunk as she was. I harnessed my mouth. I said, "I have no closet. You know all there is to know about me. It's all out there. It's all in you."

My wife said: "What have I gotten from you?"

To a new man who had seated himself beside her, my wife said, "A smoke if you've got it."

I didn't know what to tell her. Was I supposed to begin a catalog list? And of what? Of all she already knew about me? I searched for the beginning of a thread. I unwound a spool never reaching a frayed tip. When I didn't respond, my wife, distracted, said: "My eyes hurt. I need a tic-tac." She rifled through her purse, two fingers clasping the newly lit cigarette, until she found a pack of mint tic-tacs. She popped one into her mouth, grimaced at the mixture of mint, nicotine and vodka. "I found one of the love letters you wrote me when we first met." She pronounced the word "first" with a delicate slur. "You had written it in pencil," she said, "so I erased it."

I stared, appalled. "Really?" I asked. She sucked on her tic-tac. She inhaled deeply. She sipped her vodka. She crunched down.

The moment grew immense.

Nothing was wrong.

I asked my wife, "Why would you do that?"

The bartender passed and to him my wife said: "Could I get a cocktail glass of cherries?" When he nodded, squeezing a few spears of bright red into the glass, my wife said, "You're a doll. Thanks a million." My wife was some brassy moll all of a sudden, playing a part.

My wife pulled a cherry from its stem, chewed it down and slipped the stem between her lips. I waited while she tried unsuccessfully to tie it. What was once titillating to watch, once nimble in appearance, was now clumsy, sloppy. I grew impatient, I asked, "Why would you erase one of my notes?"

She spat out the stem, all her grace disappearing in that moment. She said: "My eyes are blurring. I wonder if I need glasses. I've always wanted glasses." To the man beside her she said: "A smoke if you've got it." She didn't realize it was the same gentleman whom she'd asked for a cigarette only minutes before. He reached into his inner pocket, pulled the pack from his jacket, shook a cigarette half-out of the pack, and my wife pulled it loose with her mouth. He held his lighter up and flicked the wheel, his finger planted on the button. My wife leaned her cigarette into the long flame. Her cheekbones grew more angular as she inhaled. I had never been so disgusted watching a person smoke. She turned toward me to cough and popped another cherry into her mouth, discarding the stem on the bar's surface, not willing to attempt a knot again so soon. She savored the brilliant sugar.

I was impatient and alone. I felt suddenly that she was not the wife I thought she was.

My wife chewed, inhaled, opened her eyes, squinted and then stared at me, all sloppy mischief and clumsy sleight of hand.

"What closet and why would you erase my love letter? Where is this coming from?"

"You understand what I mean about the closet, and I erased it because I could. Do you think I might need reading glasses? Little Ben Franklin readers? Wouldn't I be the picture of a little granny with those?" She wanted a response. "Dearie?" she asked, in her best imitation of an old woman.

My wife gulped her vodka. She inhaled smoke deeply. She stared at me.

I had no idea what she wanted, what I was supposed to say. I tried. "Are you unhappy with me?"

"It's not that." She shook her head, for a moment staring beyond the bottles of liquor into the bar mirror. "I don't ask nearly as much of you as you ask of me. All I'm asking is that we equalize this a little. I'm not saying I want more from you."

I took a long pull on my beer. "Well, I think you've got it backwards, but let me get this straight. You want me to want less of you."

The brassy moll disappeared and she shrank before my eyes. She looked broken. She gave an almost imperceptible nod.

"How do I do that?"

"I'm pregnant."

"Cheap trick for sympathy." There was no way.

To me my wife said: "Is it?" She sipped her vodka. She waved over the bartender and said meekly: "More vodka, please."

I shook my head, placed my hand over her glass. She pushed my hand away. More insistently, she said to the bartender: "Much more vodka, please." I reached over and slid the glass out of her reach, nodding to the bartender to take it away.

She slumped into her lap. She wasn't crying. I lifted her by the shoulders. "What's in *my* closet? You can't be serious, can you? You're not pregnant. Don't play like that."

My wife looked away .

"Even if you thought you were, you aren't anymore. You've had about a gallon of vodka tonight."

My wife gasped. I lifted my hands from her, brought them to my face, began to massage the hollows above my cheekbones.

My wife shifted her eyes to mine. "I want too much of a baby. I want it to prove my life, my age. I want to forget this selfishness. I shouldn't require anything of a baby. I can't do that. I would be a terrible mother. Take it away. I don't want anything to do with it. I'll just tell its story now." She slipped another unnaturally red cherry between her lips.

Who was this woman? "What are you talking about?"

"I'm not pregnant anymore. I lied."

"Anymore? You got rid of it?" I had to look away and then I had to look back. "You didn't tell me? When did this happen? Are you crazy?" I was off my barstool. I had her by the shoulders. I had no idea what was happening. I looked away from her and around the room trying to find something familiar.

My wife pushed my hands off. She stood. "Be quiet," she said. "This is private." She grabbed my jaw in both her hands and turned my head, pulling my face down so one ear was in front of those bright red lips. "I lost it, alright? Do you like that better? I had a miscarriage. And you know what? It was for the best. I'm glad it happened because I would have done it all wrong." She paused and I tried to turn my head, but she kept me turned away, my ear close to her lips. "Sure, it's too bad, and yeah, I'm fucking *sad*. But I know it's for the better. For me. You would have been a wonderful father. I know you would have been nothing less than perfect. I'm clumsy and selfish though." Now she turned my face towards hers. I was about to say something, though what I have no idea. She put a finger to my lips, "And a sloppy, sloppy drunk." She straightened her hand, brought it back and slapped me hard across the face. "That wasn't because you did anything wrong. I wanted to know you actually felt something."

I was silent. We sat back down. My wife asked the bartender for two glasses of water. He slid them toward us. We sipped like children, avoided eye contact.

"I'm sorry." I said.

"Shhh."

"What can I…"

"Shhh."

My tongue was a punching bag, returning every time, a muscle I slung around with an anxious lack of dignity.

I wished I could crawl on my hands and knees away from her. Instead I clutched my cup of water and waited.

I imagined we might be silent for days, communicating through slight shifts in focus or twitches of the mouth.

I was wrong. When I drained my water, she downed hers. I thought we'd head home silently, but she pushed the cups toward the bartender to refill them, then met my eyes, with softness, with weariness, and yet with resolve. "You deserve this story more than my closet does. I thought I might be pregnant a couple weeks ago. I waited. I bought four or five pregnancy tests. I stopped drinking and smoking for a short time. I waited another week. I took the tests. All positive. I wanted to keep it to myself for a few days. I was nervous. I didn't know how I felt. No matter what I knew I wanted a few days alone with the idea. I wanted to be sure what I thought before I spoke it out loud. I decided I needed to keep it. I'd never forgive myself if I ran away from something so huge. I didn't know if I wanted to raise it though. I knew if I kept it, it might become my little puppet. I might use it. It might be a toy I got to form, dress up, one more thing I got to control. Grownups can hold their own with me, but a baby I could make do whatever I wanted. A child would mean more power than I should be allowed.

"I was going to tell you when you came home from work that day. I watched you get up and get dressed, and I was nervous as I watched you leave because I knew that I had to tell you when you came home. I went back to sleep exhausted by that idea. I woke up aching in a patch of my own blood. I hadn't even seen a doctor to confirm what the store-bought tests told me, but I scheduled an emergency appointment anyway.

"It was true. I'd miscarried. They took blood. They gave me a full examination. The doctor told me I would feel good as new in a day or two. I'd only been pregnant about six weeks. He gave me the number of some counselors. I came home and I cried all day for something I hadn't even wanted.

"The cramps were gone by late afternoon, and you weren't home by the time I was supposed to go to work. I shouldn't have gone in, but I thought if I went to work I might be able to pull myself together before I saw you. I thought maybe I never had to tell you what had gone on. I thought you would be angry I hadn't told you as soon as I knew I was pregnant. I thought if I could save you from that it would be better.

"By the time I got home I had a handle on things and I tried my hardest to behave as if nothing had happened. Yesterday in the morning I began looking through old sentimental stuff I've saved. I found your old love letters and I found the one written in pencil and it hit me that only you would have written a letter in pencil, and I got an overwhelming urge to erase it. Something had been taken from me that I had no control over and I wanted to get rid of something by myself. I wanted something that had a bit of both of us and that letter was perfect. You wrote it and it was for me. It was mine to do with as I pleased and right then I wanted to destroy something you had given me before it could escape.

"Today all I wanted was to get you drunk and to learn some deep secret I hated to know about you, so I could tell you mine and make an even trade. All I wanted was to discover that you'd been frightened to tell me something, that there was something you never wanted me to know, but of course you have nothing. You do give every bit of yourself to me and you expect the same of me, and I try, but I still want to grab some things and pack them into my cheeks for some famine when I know I'll be alone and need them."

We were both silent for a long time. I searched myself, wanting to find something awful, some dark secret to offer her, but I couldn't get past everything she'd shared with me. "I wish you would have told me earlier."

She stood. "Why don't we dance?"

I pulled her hand down, so she'd sit back on the barstool. "No. I don't want to dance. You don't want to either. You just don't know what to say. Why don't we go home?"

She nodded and gathered her purse. I lifted her jacket from the back of her stool and held it up behind her so that she could easily slip her arms through the sleeves. I spun her around and buttoned her up as well. I ran my hands through the short length of her hair, brought her forehead to my lips and kissed her lightly there.

"We'll be alright." I held the door open, and while lightly pressing my hand on the small of her back, my wife passed in front of me, into the cool night.

35.

SOON AFTER MY WIFE LEFT I wrote her a letter. I wrote her a letter I knew she would never receive. I wrote it so that I would remember exactly how I felt right after she left me.

I knew it was going to appear overblown if read in hindsight, but I knew it was the honest expression of that moment. I knew the immediacy of the letter, how close to the situation it was, I knew how this would resonate even a year later. I would appear to be a mad man, angry and inordinately wronged.

I wrote the letter for all of these reasons. I wrote this letter hoping an address might commit the impossibility of appearing so that I might mail it.

I sealed the envelope and put her name on it. I carefully penned the return address and put on a stamp, a stamp that is now a few cents away from being the proper postage.

I left the address blank because I had no idea of where she was. I knew I was never going to find her again and that even if somehow I did, I would still not have anything to write in that silent spot on the envelope. If I met her again I would become immediately disoriented. I would be so eager to never release her from my sight that my eyes would stay tightly focused on her. I would never know where I was again.

I wrote her a letter that was vicious and hurtful and honest about exactly what I felt toward her.

I dug in deep, I pressed my foot against the top edge of the dirtiest spade I owned, my ballpoint pen. I stomped on that shovel until it was full of earth and grime, and I brought it all to light and deposited it on a page in a crumbling heap, filthy but appropriate, baroque, incoherent and sick:

To my lovely wife,

I wish you were here right now so I could give you a slew of gifts for what you have put me through.

I would give you a needlepoint pillow sewn with the hair of cancerous children, a woven pattern of hopeful eyes, stitched from the spoils of their war.

I would give your fingertips the discovery of the mound of a lump under your breast's fatty tissue, coated with layers of Vaseline indented with the ripped tips of fungal fingernails.

I would give you the pinching twitter of lice scrambling your scalp gnawing your bubblegum dandruff, popping bubbles that cause your hair to mat with insect vomit.

I would give you the iron taste of blood in your mouth, only after you've noticed the INFECTED sticker clinging to the outside of the bag.

I give you the musky smoked scent of our miscarried child's remains smeared from your thighs to your tits in triumph.

I give you the drag of your old soul records, played slowly and melted into the quiver of a dirge, the low death rattle of the recently deceased singing for companionship in their demise.

I am made ill by the thought of you. By the way in which I believed we belonged and functioned together. I gag at the thought of the love I thought you had for me.

I miss you. I've found bruises under my skin, now, weeks after you've gone missing, that stagnate and wait for you to heal them to a clean clarity of flesh, instead of corrupted purple and green stains that anchor themselves in the depth of my tissue.

I'm not sorry I said what I've said. I may look back on this and think it extreme, but it is truth.

I am going to assume your absence is your *truth.*

I wish I would have known. I am furious and I still love you.

Since you are gone I am going to claim you as my own. Maybe someone else is busy claiming you for themselves right now.

I don't care. I assume the you *that was mine will never be anyone else's. Maybe I'm naïve. Maybe you are simply a pattern.*

May you replicate with agility and grace. May you compound steadily, simplifying infrequently and only out of necessity.

I will write you letters the way a young lover whispers his secrets to a scarecrow loudly enough for his lover nearby to overhear.

Eavesdrop.

Love,

Your husband

I hated writing this letter and yet it made me feel better. I knew she would never read it and yet the cruel act of voicing such terrible thoughts was enough for me.

I could have gone on, but this was my concentrated worst and I wanted her nauseated.

I repeat that I knew she would never read this letter.

But I imagined instances in which she would.

I imagined her on a Greyhound bus next to a child who had demanded the window seat. I imagined her turning away to throw up in the aisle at the thought of what I'd written. I imagined her vomit splattering the lap of an elderly woman seated across the aisle from her. I imagined her throwing the letter into the puddle in an attempt to erase it before she could read the rest. I imagined waves of her remorse at leaving me flooding through, weaving her with surging nausea.

I imagined her at the bottom of a lake, still and bloated, watching the letter float before her eyes. I imagined her waterlogged fingers clumsily fumbling the letter open. I imagined the moment her eyes fell upon the first abuse was when her eye sockets dilated to a slackness that set her eyeballs loose to float a bit in front of her face. I imagined those eyes reaching toward the letter, not believing what they were reading. I imagined the loosely ballooning skin of her mouth opened wide in horror and apology. I imagined her floating to the surface, letting the tide drag her to shore, any landmass being that much closer to me.

But mostly, I imagined an instance in which some distantly renowned god had turned her into a statue so that she might become eternal and universal. I imagined her missing an arm, perhaps a dent in the stone where her nose once was. I imagined smooth planes where the age she wanted had worn away what few curves she had, sanded them down to mere angles. I imagined her old in an ancient sort of way that would have pleased her immensely. I imagine her a caryatid, one arm still raised above her head supporting nothing more than air, air and sky, and at night, when viewed from the right angle, resting in her palm: one star shining so clearly it must have burnt out already, its light still on its journey to earth's eyes. I imagine her situated in a museum, salvaged and displayed in a courtyard. I imagine one guard slipping out into the garden on his rounds. I imagine him looking from side to side, checking to make sure none of the other guards were passing through the windowed corridors inside. I imagine him placing my letter onto the stretched tall palm of her hand. I watch his face shift as he walks away as if he has done nothing out of the ordinary, his usual disinterest shifting back into his features. I imagine the guard letting himself back into the museum proper with his heavy ring of keys. I imagine him thoroughly locking off the corridor again, and glancing out to make sure the letter still lies on my wife's palm.

Only when no human eyes rest on her any longer does the statue of my wife feel the weight of my letter in her hand. She cannot bring her arm down; it is made of stone. Even if she could bend she has no other arm and hand with which she might open the letter. She can only feel the great heaviness of my sentiments funneled into words, deposited onto paper, wrapped into an envelope. She cannot know precisely what they say, can only feel the burden anchoring her shoulder into its socket, heavier than any ruin's lintel she has before hefted high above her head.

It is as this statue that I desire my wife to receive my missive. I would never wish the words I wrote to cross anyone's line of sight, but if there were a way that she could know the nature and tonnage of my message without having to read the words, I would wish this fate upon her; I would wish her a weight for eternity as heavy as the one she placed on me, one which might only be worn down by the whipping sands of time.

I can think of no more accurate instance of retribution, but age and weight.

36.

My wife helped to decorate a local haunted house each fall.

She was in charge of one room and it seemed to be the favorite attraction of most of the patrons. It looked like a work of art.

My wife scoured flea markets and antique shops year round, always with a purpose lurking in the back of her mind to hunt up broken dolls and masks that she could use in the haunted house.

The room she designed was bathed in red light. The ceiling was covered in dry branches and leaves. Stapled to the walls were all of the dolls and masks, many missing arms, many naked, many lacking half of a face, shirred or with one eye glued shut from moisture and time.

The dolls hung in all sizes: ventriloquist dummies, Madame Alexander dolls, life-size plastic little boys, baby dolls, voodoo dolls, stuffed animal people. The masks were African tribal masks, deflated rubber costume masks, ceramic masquerade masks.

In the room, visitors were terrified and overwhelmed by the sense that they were being watched.

In the center of the room she hung one of the most lifelike dummies I've ever seen.

It was the body of a naked, middle-aged woman. She hung in a noose and her feet dangled about a foot above the ground. Beneath her was a pile of chicken bones, delicate and in danger of being crushed when the woman was inevitably cut down.

The scene made no real sense, but when one walked into the room, there was a petrifying, eerie feeling. It seemed like the woman was hanging there because of all the eyes that were trained on her. None of the eyes looked nearly as real as the body that was hanging in the middle of the room.

Everything felt slightly false.

This falseness felt like part of the problem.

When people were going through the haunted house, a lot of monsters and ghosts jumped out to surprise them, but when they came to this room, the stillness was overwhelming. People would stand waiting for something to happen, but the more nothing happened the faster their hearts started to beat, and the more they wanted to leave the room. They had paid to be scared though, and so they stayed as long as they could and then left, perhaps disappointed that nothing had ever grabbed them or fallen on them, but also undeniably affected.

When I asked my wife where the idea had come from, what it all meant, she seemed reluctant to reveal anything.

"It's about seeing and being seen."

"It's about pressure and shame."

And then her mood would shift. "It's a haunted house room. It's not about anything."

Each time she changed her answer, and each time I told her how scared I had been, precisely because of the stillness and the illogic of the details. In all of the other rooms you could figure out the stereotypical creepy situation, but in this one the unknown was deafening in its silence.

My wife said, "To be someone else. To play games one doesn't know the rules for. Delightful, isn't it? Halloween is a time for make-believe and pretend and the unknown. My room lets Halloween be what it wants to be, not what people expect of it."

37.

MY WIFE LAUGHED OFF her tumbles because it was like a conscious reminder that she had to slow down. She had to stop and think occasionally which foot she was going to put in front of the other.

It was like she was catching up with herself.

My wife would pick herself up and dust herself off.

My wife would keep going.

As she walked away she would examine the heels of her hands, callused and scarred over.

"You shouldn't catch yourself like that," I would tell her again and again. "You'll break something someday."

She would dust out bits of gravel, look up at me wide-eyed, and shake her head.

38.

WHEN I TRY TO THINK about what she was to me, it's both easy to come up with answers and complicated.

I had a dream that I was a child and I had a pet dodo bird. I had no way of effectively leashing this bird except to tie a piece of bread to a string and feed the bread to the dodo, the other end of the string still in my hand. Then, I could pull the gagging bird along with me. In the dream, my mother yells at me to stop doing this if I truly love the bird. My fear is that it will escape. I feed it this way again and again and it eventually kills the bird.

When I recall the time my wife and I had together, I think about how happy I was, but I can also admit that happiness is relative and, if I look for it, I find I can enjoy being alone. I would never have predicted this, and, more importantly, never wished it. She was my life and I still haven't figured out what I am without her.

I have only these guarded memories I roll around in my hands again and again. They are no doubt getting tarnished, but they seem bright as ever. We spent our time alone together, with the exception of the rare strangers my wife befriended. They couldn't have known her like I did, and perhaps that's the point: that it was only me who knew her that way. Who is there to try and talk me out of this vision of her I hold so close?

When I opened that closet door, and pressed "play" again and again for each and every tape that sat in that closet, I heard nothing. Every one of those stories she had taken the time to relay was gone. It was shocking to hear the silence. Each carefully labeled case, filled with a thin cassette, was empty. Like mug shots with no film in the camera, each person had been scrutinized from multiple angles, and then released into the night, untraceable.

39.

Just weeks before I would see her for the last time, we walked through a prairie up north. My shoes were soaked through with dew in minutes and I stepped carefully to avoid actual puddles and muddy low points in the trail. My wife splashed ahead, galoshes barring the moisture from her feet. She was safe.

"Wait up, Speedy!" I called, sidestepping a pile a stray dog had left behind. She turned her head before she darted down the left fork in the path. I resigned myself to the sloshing feeling and jogged to catch up. When I reached her she was on a bridge, sturdy, but swaying back and forth. She was shifting her weight, enjoying the ride.

"Whoa. Wobbly," I said, and as my first step landed on the bridge, she started moving more violently. I almost lost my balance, but I steadied myself on the cable handrails. She smiled at me devilishly and walked calmly off the bridge. "What was that about?" I asked, still a little shaken.

"A test," she replied, seriously. I searched her face, and, looking back, the resignation was there then. A decision had been made and it had little to do with how I reacted to her swaying a bridge. Whatever she had decided was a long time coming and had more to do with her than anyone else.

"Well, you know, 'Be prepared!'" I stopped for a moment as she ran ahead again. I wanted to look out at all of the ground we'd covered. It was a crisp fall day and we'd come north along the lakeshore to some open prairielands to admire the leaves changing and take in the fresh air. Winter would be upon us soon. We'd be housebound and hermetic, frozen by the fact of it. At that moment I thought about turning around and heading back. If I left, my wife would be lost. I knew she was counting on me to keep track of the path we'd taken. She'd gone ahead, and who knew how far? I could walk back at my leisurely pace enjoying myself and it might be hours before she found her way back to where we'd parked the car. The grass was high and it was impossible to predict which way a certain fork would lead. I looked in the direction she'd headed and looked back from where we came and decided I couldn't do it. She would be angry and could possibly get herself hurt out here on her own with her clumsiness and poor sense of direction.

I stood where I was, waiting, and finally she returned, giving me a look that both asked why I hadn't followed and answered the same question. She looked out from the vantage point at which I'd positioned myself. She stood in front of me, her back against my stomach, her head against my shoulder. I hugged her. "Look at all of this. It's huge."

"I hope you remember where we've come from because I am *lost*," she said.

"I know how to get back," I replied. "I've been keeping close track. I kissed the top of her head and thanked goodness that she returned to me so we could look out together. In seconds, the wind started up again and we were off.

Years later, I'm still searching my memory for my wife. I find her now and again in unexpected places, and it's there I feel like I know who I am. In the relief of rediscovering her, I'm able to place myself within her, about her.

40.

I CALLED MY WIFE'S ART teacher. We had never spoken, but in the midst of the mess, in the aftermath of her departure, I found a registration form for the class. I filed it away.

I'd never heard one of her recordings. I'd never seen her painting. I'd stopped trying to reason her out and was simply waiting for signals. I had been trained by the end; I knew and performed the appropriate reactions.

I had stopped trying to connect dots, because the dots weren't numbered. There was an infinite quantity of paths between points the lines could take.

My wife was a constellation without a mythology to inform her shapes.

I wondered about that still life, that painting she had never let me see, because her teacher had heard sounds from within the canvas that couldn't be seen.

I wanted to see it, to try to experience my own jumbled version of perception.

So I called her teacher. When I'd regrouped the apartment; when I'd taken photographs of the state of things immediately after she left; when I'd begun to be able to talk in less tangents; when my speech patterns had resumed their normal linear paths and I was no longer punctuating each conversation with questions of grief and confusion, I called her teacher and I asked for that painting.

He said he would never part with it. It was a work of art, and he suspected it would be worth a lot of money some day.

I explained to him what had happened, that my wife had disappeared, and he apologized, said he wondered why he hadn't heard from her. He didn't offer up the painting though.

"I need this," I said to this man, but saying such a naked statement to someone who does not know you, someone who has no idea how difficult it is to say something like that, saying something like "I need this" in the most honest and vulnerable way you can muster, never quite has the effect you would hope. It's easy to deny the unknown.

This man was obviously staying on the line for the sake of politeness; it was not because he was going to reconsider. I changed my tactic. "Can I come and look at the painting?"

The man exhaled on the other end of the line. I imagined his eyes flicking around the room trying to think of any reason he could give me so that he would no longer have to deal with the situation, looking for some excuse as to why he might not have to allow me anywhere near his office or his home or his classroom, or wherever it was that he was housing my wife's painting at the moment. Finally, "I'm not sure your wife would want me to do that."

The tense of his statement brought me to tears. I thought this would be easier and that I would have the strength to make it through a simple phone call without breaking down. I had already begun to refer to her in the past tense. Despite my belief that I was going to be able to recover her, I had to let myself believe that she was gone. "It doesn't matter what she would

want you to do now. She's not here anymore and—" I didn't
want to say it. I didn't want to say it because it felt irreversible
and I didn't want to say it because it would be bigger than I was
able to handle. I didn't want to say it because I knew if I did, I
would have said it as a tool to get to see this painting, and, for
that same reason, I wanted to say it. I wanted to say it and have
him break down and offer the painting to me. I wanted to say it
and then force myself to deal with it, and so I said it: "She's not
coming back."

The art teacher didn't know me. He hadn't heard all that
reasoning that went on in my head before I said that irrevocable
statement that meant all my hope was gone, that the reason I
wanted to see that painting was not because I thought it would
bring her back. The reason I wanted to see that painting was for
myself. I wanted to see what she wouldn't show me. I wanted it
to lead me to her, but the "her" I knew was never meant for me.
I wanted it to lead me to her, but I didn't think it was going to
bring her back.

I realized then what I thought I would find in this painting
was some sort of one-way mirror through which I could catch a
glimpse of her without her knowing I was there.

But the art teacher didn't know all this. He said, "You
shouldn't give up hope just yet. How long has she been gone?
Two, three weeks? She'll probably show up from some tropical
vacation, refreshed and- and- oblivious to the fact that you
would have been worrying about her. If she calls me up and says
it's alright if you see the painting, I'll be happy to show you, but
I can't show it to you right now. Sorry, pal." And this time he
did hang up.

I held the phone receiver in my hand for a long time. And I
realized that he had not known my wife because the idea that she
would go off to the Caribbean by herself was inane. In comparison,
it seemed rational that she would disappear for good.

I had worried that my wife had told him not to let me see the painting if I ever asked. I had wondered what my wife had told him about me. I became nervous that he knew something I didn't. I wanted to see that painting because I thought it would fill me in. I thought all that he knew of her must be in that painting and I wanted it all.

I went to the school and found his office. "She's not here and she's not coming back and I know this for a fact and I don't find this easy to say or even think, so take my word for it and let me see the painting. I need something here: I'm lost without her and I need *something*. This is all I can think of."

Once I stopped speaking I allowed myself to register the man I was talking to. He was larger, older and hairier than I was. He sat at a desk littered with a mess comparable to that which had decorated my apartment for the last two weeks. He had an immense bookshelf behind him filled with big, expensive books and unidentifiable objects that appeared to be abstract modern sculptures. He looked at me, eyebrows raised, but not entirely put off by my presence.

He cleared his throat, adjusted his position in his chair, and looked me straight in the eye. "I'll let you look at it, but you are not taking that picture out of here and if you give me any trouble I *will* call security."

This response seemed extreme, but I agreed. "Anything is enough right now," I said, because, at that moment, anything and something were the same thing.

He stood, tugging on the belt holding up his threadbare corduroys. "I'll be right back. I come back and it looks like you've so much as set a finger on something in here, the painting goes back into storage. Got it?" He stepped out of the door behind me and I waited.

It seemed like he was gone a long time, but when he returned he had a large canvas turned toward himself. It was about four feet tall the way he was holding it and maybe two feet wide. He came in and I tried to position myself beside him so that I could see the painting. He turned it away from me as I moved. "Ten minutes," he said. "I'll give you ten minutes and I'm not leaving the room."

I nodded and as he turned the painting to me, he shifted it so that the length of it stretched horizontally.

I stood there, calmly dumbfounded. My head began nodding immediately to the rhythm of my heavily beating heart. I knew this painting. I had already seen it.

I could feel the man watching my reaction. I knew he wanted me to begin responding out loud.

The teacher must have left the room, but I heard nothing: no footsteps down the hall, no low murmur of voices or a distant grandfather clock chiming from the canvas. If this teacher had told the truth and heard something when he looked at the painting it did not do this for me. The painting seemed entirely quiet to me. There was just the muffled drumbeat nudging in my chest that even this painting could not drown out.

This *still life* was a painting of a room. It was a destroyed room. There were holes torn into the walls. A mattress stretched, up-ended toward the corners of the room. It looked as if a snake had sidled through the space, shedding many years' layers of colorful cotton skin. Cracked ceramics punctuated these stretches of sleeve and sheet carpeting the floor. Drawers were pulled free and stood on their ends, their contents littered and tangled and cracked in lumps. The whole scene looked correct.

This painting was our apartment the day she left.

I have the distinct feeling that looking at that painting my face did not change. I feel certain that my expression had paralyzed as soon as the canvas was flipped round. I knew my head nodded, agreeing with everything I was seeing, affirming that yes it was true. She was gone and she wasn't coming back and this painting had known before I knew. She had whispered this information with her brushstrokes, had revised her plan laying layers of paint on each other, compounding them into a literal vision of where she could see our future was headed.

She had said with paint, had told this canvas, what words couldn't say, what she couldn't tell me.

I stared at the painting and the old questions forked into new ones. Had she thought of destroying the apartment, of leaving, and then painted this, hoping it would satisfy that urge? Or had she painted this and seen how attractive an option such destruction proved? Either way the similarity between this painting and the damage done to our apartment, as well as the time that had elapsed between the creation of both, proved that she had spent time thinking about it. She hadn't made a rash decision. Our apartment hadn't been torn apart while she was kidnapped. What she had done to our home, the fact that she was gone, this painting was the link between then and now and every confused moment before and to come.

I stared at the painting and the *why* of the whole situation was not answered, and the *where* didn't even seem relevant.

"Time's up."

I looked away and the art teacher began to spin the painting back to himself.

"Thank you," I said, and because it was honest and I felt compelled to say something else, "That helped a lot."

"Goodbye, then." He was waiting for me to step from his office so he could do the same, so he could put the painting back in storage.

I stepped tentatively from the room and he hustled out after me. He shut the door behind him. I walked through the exit, got in my car and drove back to the apartment.

My home looks pristine now, untouched by my wife, clean of her wreckage.

41.

MY WIFE WALKED OUT of theatres when she was bored, offended, tired, felt like moving.

I sat through every movie I ever bought a ticket to, even if they were insufferable. I waited to see how a story turned out, if it redeemed itself. If my wife was sufficiently offput halfway through something, she saw no reason to continue, to give it more of a chance.

She felt no obligation to anyone or anything.

My wife acted and reacted with meticulous consideration of herself. I see now, though, it was not often that she considered what her actions would spur in others. She behaved for herself alone, and I was the one who most tolerated this behavior. I was in such awe of her, so ready to be filled by her, that I rarely questioned a thing. She was who I had the most faith in and she was my faith itself, a conduit through which I lived my life. Everything was once removed through her.

There is a large part of me through which I still channel that way of life. When I think about her leaving I can transfer back to those strong feelings of sympathy. When she first left I felt the need to imagine myself in her place and imagine why she must have done whatever it was she did.

In this realm I can feel certain as my wife pulled drawers from dressers that she owned each movement. I can be sure that as she swept her arm through the kitchen cupboard she committed to what she was doing and had a vague idea of why she moved her arm with the force she did.

I can be sure that the day my wife climbed the stairs up to our apartment so that she could tear it apart, she felt the weight of Sisyphus. I'm sure as she stumbled up the stairs she felt like she was hauling her history for the millionth time. I can have no doubt that as she came nearer our apartment's floor, the heft of her history grew more burdensome and she tripped under the pressure.

It makes me nauseous to think of the degree to which I am still capable of snapping back into this mode of thinking, of justification.

I can still quite easily imagine that when my wife flung the door open, this action was the most liberating she'd ever taken. When she had reached the top of her mountain the slight plateau of its peak certainly allowed the force she exerted on her load to lessen a bit and so that door flying open would be something like the last push that breaks into a moment of no resistance.

My wife must have felt light, dancing about the apartment and tearing down what had rooted her for so long. I imagine she cried tears of joy, then glanced in fear at the door when she heard footsteps reaching our landing, and I imagine she stood still for a long time in front of the closet and considered what to do.

But it wasn't that she was worrying about me, or about how I would react when I figured out she was gone, or how I would cope when she, the woman through which I had lived, was absent. She wasn't thinking about what she must have known, that without her now, after all this time, I would feel like a ghost. She was thinking about how, if I had walked in at that moment, that moment would be less perfect because it wouldn't have fit as neatly into her grand design.

Right after she left, what I would imagine most was how she must have descended that staircase.

I believed my wife must have flown. Finally stripped of every truth she had been trapped within, I imagined my wife was nude and lithe and gliding back down to the earth again. I imagined the stairs carried her smoothly so she didn't have to bother with the graduated treads of the staircase. Maybe the stairs leaned into themselves creating a slide she could ride to the ground floor.

My wife was setting herself so free.

She allowed herself none of the limits of the nostalgia she had for so long defined herself by.

Armed only with her aging hands, she must have pulled the door shut behind her and paused.

My wife must have realized exactly what she was doing and, in a moment, she must have decided to forget.

For so long I had imagined my wife as this woman who had lived trying to remember not for herself, but for everyone else, and when I thought of her leaving, I imagined that she must have paused a moment and left it all behind.

Her hand closed around the doorknob; her arm pulled the door shut and she turned to lock the apartment from the outside.

My wife slid the key in the lock, turned it, and then slipped down the stairs.

The one truth I know is that I came home.

I climbed the stairs, light and unknowing.

I slid my own key into the lock, turned and pushed.

ACKNOWLEDGMENTS

Grateful acknowledgment is made to the following publications in which portions of this novel first appeared: *The Denver Quarterly, Wigleaf, Melusine,* and *Mud Luscious.*

Many thanks, in no particular order, to Matt Bell, Dan Wickett, Steven Gillis, Jennifer Hancock, Beth Nugent, Carol Anshaw, Bin Ramke, Janet Desaulniers, Steven Seighman and Amanda Jane Jones.

Thanks to the Ragdale Foundation and Vermont Studio Center for time and space, and to my classmates at the School of the Art Institute of Chicago.

Above all, thanks to my family and friends for their love, support and tolerance, especially Mom, Dad, Jenny and Jared.